Finnegan's Wind

JOHN WOOD

WOLFHOUND PRESS

First published in 2000 by
Wolfhound Press Ltd
68 Mountjoy Square
Dublin 1, Ireland
Tel: (353-1) 874 0354
Fax: (353-1) 872 0207

The Arts Council
An Chomhairle Ealaíon

Wolfhound Press receives financial assistance from The Arts
Council/An Chomhairle Ealaíon, Dublin, Ireland.

British Library Cataloguing in Publication Data
A catalogue record for this book is available from the British Library.

ISBN 0-86327-831-0

10 9 8 7 6 5 4 3 2 1

Cover Illustration: Angela Clarke
Cover Design: Wolfhound Press
Typesetting: Wolfhound Press
Printed in the UK by Cox & Wyman Ltd, Reading, Berks.

To Mr Compton, our local pig farmer,
for telling me things about pigs I did not know —
or, rather, things I did not know about pigs ... my thanks.
To the memory of Mr George of Tripes Farm,
whose pigs I often heard and smelt in a west wind, many years ago;
to the ghosts of those gypsies who once travelled the lanes ...
my respects.
To Jan, my wife, to whom this book is dedicated ... my love.

1

High up, brushed by the clouds, they were bumping along a narrow road through the rocks and heather. Then it twisted off the moor to the green valleys and ridges lower down. At last they were off the wilderness and on their way to Mr Finnegan's.

There were people here — there were farms and villages; fields of wheat pocketed amongst the trees; flocks of pigeons, blue and still, feeding in the corn; fast-running rivers. And Callum shivered.

It was to be a new home for the Wards. A new place. And with it, as always for Callum, came a whiff of uncertainty.

They were nearly there. According to Aaron Ward, who was driving the lorry, they were, anyway. Strictly speaking, it was not a new home; it was a chicken hut, with a few droppings still in it, to be put up in a new place. Callum, squeezed against his sister in the passenger seat, was thinking of the last place: a paddock, with wild uncut hedges.

Callum would not be telling his classmates at school that he was a traveller. Sometimes he would get to the top of the class — which he usually did — before they found out.

Neither Callum nor Kate had seen the new place, but their father had scouted the site days earlier and found it satisfactory. And this had been impressed upon both of them: even a hut — if you live in it — is a home.

Callum wriggled against Kate, pushing his elbows out, as he thought of the new school, of the teasing — although sometimes the children just kept away from him when they found out what he was. He usually kept silent, but once he'd answered: 'We're as free as the wind!' It was something his father had said. Callum did not believe in crying.

Kate pinched his arm. 'Stop pressing,' she said.

The lorry was packed with the dismantled hut — the sides and ends and roof section — and with bedding, cases, beds, pots and pans, lamps, a can of kerosene, a box of mice with air-holes punched in it, and one or two other odds and ends, all covered with tarpaulin and tied down tight. Mrs Ward — Phoebe to those who knew her — sat at the back, on a bundle of clothes, with the tarpaulin propped up over her head.

They had turned down a high-banked lane alongside a wood where the shadows milled. It was so narrow that the ferns and foxgloves brushed against both sides.

'Go carefully!' shouted Phoebe, suddenly fearful.

Then, being unheard, she started banging the tail-board with a broom handle.

Kate gazed out of the window as they stopped. She tried to shift away from Callum.

'What's up with Mum now?' she said, but more to herself.

Aaron leaned out, pushing the bracken away from his face, and called back, 'What is it, Ma?'

'Go carefully, I said.'

'We're nearly there.'

'All the more reason, then.'

Aaron turned to Kate, frowning. 'Your ma's tired, that's what,' he said.

Then, a few moments later, he recognised the track leading into the wood and swung into it without braking. He managed to pull over into a clearing among the trees, well off the road, just as the lorry's wheels started to spin.

'This is it,' he said.

Phoebe, looking tired and sucking a boiled sweet, and seeming rounder than usual because she was wearing two cotton dresses on account of the draughts at the back, had started walking about on the soft pine needles.

'It's me legs,' she said, stretching them. Her full cheeks were mottled with anxiety; her eyes had grown large and wary.

A few bats were on the wing. Pigeons had gathered on the top of an oak, getting ready for their evening roost. The quiet was intense.

'This could make a nice place for a home,' she said.

'We'll have to look sharp if we want to be set up by nightfall,' said Aaron. 'Me and Ma'll work on the shed. You, both of you, know what to do. And Kate, let Callum alone — how many more times must I tell you? And you, my son, don't stand there dreaming!'

And he was, it was true. Of the last village school. Of the other children being collected in Volvos ... not that he minded that. But they were going back to sitting-rooms; kitchens; real bedrooms; to gardens with rhubarb and potatoes and flowers and dead spiders in the greenhouse ... that sort of thing.

~

Soon the fire in the clearing was alight, blazing with the fallen wood that Callum had collected in the darkening forest. As he looked at the sticks whistling and bubbling with hot sap, he prayed that the Ward family would find happiness here. A smoke-blackened pot hung on chains suspended from iron legs. Already steam was rising.

Phoebe asked, 'Water nice and clean, was it?'

Kate, who had fetched it, nodded.

'Wouldn't have chosen here, otherwise,' said Aaron, 'seeing as running water is a necessity.'

'You call that running water, Dad?' It was Kate, smiling to herself.

'Yes, it is, my girl, in the sense that your father means it,' Phoebe replied.

'What's for supper, Ma?' asked Callum.

'First things first,' Phoebe said. 'Now, how about a cup of tea? Then I was wondering about that last bit of pork.... How about that, everybody?'

'Or we could have bacon,' said Callum.

'The pork needs eating up. And you know how I feel about bacon at the moment,' said Phoebe. 'We've bacon hanging up, curing, all over the place. I've put the curtains up in the hut, made the beds, put fresh

candles in, and what else have I done? I've hung up
those hams! It's not natural.'

'It's going to take ages,' said Callum.

'We don't have a cooker at present, Callum; it was
destroyed, as you well know. We'll have tea, like I said;
the kettle's ready. Then I'll put the pork in the pot....'

'How long, Mum?' he persisted. 'I'm starving.'

'I don't doubt it. But you'll have to wait, won't you?'
Phoebe said. 'It's got to be boiled a bit first, then
roasted over the flames.'

Firelight flickered on their faces; on the great fir
branches which swept down to the ground, almost en-
circling them. The sun had dipped below the horizon.

'We can't carry on like this,' Phoebe said.

Aaron said, 'It'll get better.'

'What's going to happen in the winter?' asked Kate.

'She means we're going to get frozen, living in an 'ut,'
said Phoebe, 'designed and built with chickens in mind.'

'If it hadn't been for the kindness of that lady giving
us the hut....' Aaron said.

'Obliging some poor chicken to find other quarters,'
interrupted Phoebe.

'Mum,' said Kate, 'who cares about the chickens?
Those villagers burned down our caravan. That's what
matters.'

'Come on, this won't do — us going on at each
other,' said Phoebe. 'It'll be better here; I can feel it
already. Make the tea, Katie, there's a good girl. And
look: your pa's upset. Callum, go in the 'ut and bring
out the pillows to warm up.'

With Aaron looking quietly at the flames, Callum
held each of the four pillows in turn against the heat,
and he felt the moisture from them rise into his face
like spiderwebs.

'Don't worry, Dad,' said Callum. 'We'll have enough money for another caravan soon. It stands to reason. You're the best pig-man around.'

'When we've seen to Mr Finnegan's pigs, we'll be in the money, all right,' said Aaron, 'especially seeing that I'll be looking after the swill-making side of things, as well.'

'All those innards,' Phoebe complained.

'It's not like that, you know it isn't. We don't just use innards. It's whole chickens ... those the food factories don't want.'

'They've got innards in,' persisted Phoebe, 'and more than likely they've gone off.'

'How many times have I told you, Ma? Plate-waste from the hospitals and hotels is smellier than anything, especially if there's cabbage in it. But there's a pie factory near here.'

'What good is that?'

'Trimmings,' said Aaron.

'But you'll come home smelly,' she said.

'It's part of the trade; you know that,' Aaron replied. 'But anyway, he said I can wash at his place. He said all of us can.'

'He sounds very reasonable, this Mr Finnegan,' said Phoebe.

Aaron asked, 'How much longer for supper, Ma?'

'Oh, don't you start!'

'A couple of hours?'

She nodded.

'I could be back by then.... There's plenty of pigs about, and you said this was the last of the fresh pork.'

'Surely you're not going to take one of Mr Finnegan's?' Phoebe protested.

'Have I ever done such a thing?'

'Dad wouldn't,' said Callum.

'No, I suppose not. Off you go, then, dear, if you must.... Supper will be ready when you come back. There's no point in me trying to stop you, but this time a little one, please, so that we can have all of it fresh over the next few days. Can't stand the thought of salting more hams. So a young one, please. It'll make better crackling, anyway. And Callum likes his crackling, don't you, Callum boy?'

Aaron said, 'Stand up and turn your back to the fire, my son. Look up. It's a good night, a clear sky and as big a harvest moon as I ever saw. There's stars to help us, and a breeze that will hold pig-smell if we're windward of them.'

Then Callum felt his father's hand so heavily on his head that he could not swivel it, and then Aaron was saying seriously — like a man out of the Bible, his voice rumbling into Callum's bones — 'It's time you understood animals, Callum boy, like me and Katie does, so's you can pull your weight down at Mr Finnegan's.'

'There'll be his school homework, Aaron, before you get any ideas.'

'So I'm taking you with me,' Aaron said, ignoring her, 'to show you how I manage pigs. Same as I hope Kate'll teach you how to understand the mice, one day.'

'Leave him be, Aaron,' said Phoebe.

'No, I won't, dear. It's a good night for a bit of piggin', and I can't miss it.'

'He means pig-stealing,' said Kate.

'No, I don't,' said Aaron. 'If we don't take it, how can it be stealing? Callum will see!'

~

'That's a nice little pig you've got there, Callum,' said Phoebe later, on their return. 'I'm blessed if it isn't. I don't know how your father does it; it beats me.'

'It's a gift,' said Aaron modestly.

'The pig doesn't like being near that pot,' said Callum.

'No more he doesn't,' agreed Aaron, pleased at his son's understanding of the pig's feelings. 'Now then, Callum boy, you and me we'll take him into the woods a short way, like I always do, eh, Ma? We shan't be long. You come behind me, Callum. You've done well, my son.'

Aaron moved easily in the scattered moonbeams, down the track towards the brook, stopping only where the bank had fallen in, for here they could walk to the water's edge.

'This will do,' said Aaron, *'won't it, my dear pig?* See what I'm doing, Callum? I'm telling it something. I'm thinking of that pig. *Perhaps you'd like to be directed to an oak tree so you can root around under it?'*

He moved out of the moonlight and back to the nearest oak, saying over his shoulder, 'If you set your mind to it, Callum, you can sense the trees in front of you. It's all to do with instinct, and allowing yourself to believe something. It's the same with pig-talk.'

The pig had followed them to the oak just as it had followed them back over the fields.

Callum put his hand out in the blackness of the wood and touched the pig's nose, and he heard a small, fleeting sound from within it — not a snort, but a signal of understanding ... and his heart leapt.

'It will stay here until morning, Callum, when all I've got to do is whistle for it — no trouble at all. You see, my son, it's to do with belief and confidence. You've got to believe what you're saying to it. Don't try too hard. Let it come natural, so's in a minute it's having confidence in you, likewise. You don't have to talk out loud, not if you don't want to. Thinking it in your head is enough — *isn't it, my beauty?*' he asked, fondling the pig round its ears and saying 'There!' every time it grunted.

'For example,' he went on, 'I've been thinking this to myself — saying it here.' Aaron tapped his head. '*I'd regard it as a special favour, pig, if you'd stay here tonight all comfortable until I fetch you in the morning. I can't tie you up, just in case we've been followed ... but you don't mind, do you?*

'You see, my son, you've got to believe that you're no better than he is. It's a wonderful feeling for both of you. It's the first time he's had real respect. He warms to you and listens, *don't you, my pig friend?*'

'All right, but what if we've been seen?'

'It's unlikely, but what if we have, my son? I've not stolen him. It's all voluntary on his part. It happened once that I was seen. Farmer said, "You've got my pig." "Blessed if you're not right," I said. "You should keep your pigs under better control."'

~

'Has he been a help, Aaron?' asked Phoebe, handing plates to the figures squatting around the fire. Although there was some flame from it still, she said, 'Go get a lamp from the 'ut, Callum.'

And then they ate in silence, except for the noise they made with the crackling, and this Callum liked more than anything; but — as he bit into the crackling and felt the sounds of it going right through his head and out of his ears — in spite of this, he was troubled about what would happen to the pig.

'That was really nice, Ma,' said Aaron, licking his fingers, knowing that the future always looked better after something to eat, and beginning also to reflect, in a comfortable sort of way, on the evening's work.

'You've got a good nose for pig-smell, my son,' he said.

'So have you,' said Kate, wishing to keep Callum in his place.

'We'll make a pig-talker of him yet,' said Aaron, 'same as Katie being a mouse-talker.'

'Not that I can do any of it,' said Phoebe.

'It's not in your genes, my pet,' said Aaron.

'The pig is very quiet. It won't have gone?' she asked. 'It's untied?'

'Of course,' said Aaron. 'I've never had a pig that's let me down and gone back of its own accord. No, it'll be there in the morning, all right. Then I'll see to it; it's a fast brook, and the blood will go away a treat.'

'Katie, you can help me salt it,' said Phoebe.

'What about Callum?' Kate asked.

'He'll be getting ready for school.'

'Oh, come on, Mum,' Callum groaned.

'Your dad fixed it all up like I asked him to, before we got here.'

'But tomorrow?' Callum protested.

'You should think yourself lucky there's a school in the village, and not complain about it. It's a pity Kate never took to it.'

'No it isn't. I went to one once — remember? — and I hated it,' Kate replied, kicking the fire.

~

Callum could not sleep.

Sometimes he was thinking of school, then of the pig-stealing. But mainly of school ... that, and reputations, and what a bad one the Wards had.

A curtain divided their sleeping quarters from their parents'. In the next bed, moonlight shone on Kate's pillow and on her face and black hair. Beside the bed, on an upturned box, was the mouse in a cage. Callum was not sure if he was being watched by it or not. Then for an instant he saw its eyes. They were no bigger than grape seeds, and curiously bright.

He thought of the journey back with the pig. He kept on going over it, and over again.

The pig had followed all the way, forcing itself through hedges as he and Aaron had climbed the moonlit stiles. And they had walked the bright fields, this strange and silent band: father and son and pig.

What madness made them do it?

How would they ever find happiness?

He was properly awake, now. He looked at Kate, listening carefully to her breathing. He prayed that the mouse would not squeak, as it often did when it wanted her attention.

Then, picking up his clothes, he moved past the space where his parents slept, taking care not to touch the curtains. He took a long time, sensing where obstacles were, turning the door handle so that it made no sound. He kicked the embers of the fire and dressed in front of it.

He went down the path, the same one that led to the brook, and got to the pig. He sat down with it and told it exactly what the situation was, and of its many dangers, and how it was to follow him back to the place it had come from, and how it would have some more life to live yet. He told it of the fast-moving brook, of the silver water lying like a scarf in the cold ground that would take its blood away.

There was not, thought Callum, much that could be done about the pig being collected in a lorry, as it would be one day. That was something that happened to pigs. But for it to be deceived, before its time had come, by a pig-talker.... And he had helped to make that bond. He had shown respect to the pig, and had been trusted. He could not allow it to happen.

'*Come on*,' he said, and off they went, with Callum getting a good whiff of distant pig-smell. He trembled with anxiety, hoping that he was headed in the right direction. Certainly he was going nowhere near Mr Finnegan's. He told the pig to have patience, and he apologised for taking him in the first place.

All this he was able to do with confidence; for, unknown to the rest of the family, he had for a long time been able to talk to pigs and mice. He could talk to most animals. That is, he understood their feelings very well.

2

Callum struggled to free himself of the madness of that walk. The moonlight! ... the way it turned the hedges into foundering ships, owls into dead mariners! Never, for him, had there been such a night before. It was like a dream. The only part of it which seemed real was his reason for doing it.

Again his mother called: 'Come and get your breakfast, or you'll be late for school.'

Aaron was kneeling down in the clearing, moving a sharpening stone across the blade of his butcher's knife. He was like Callum, thin and restless, his skin the colour of a travelling man's.

'Here, put this on,' said Phoebe, throwing a green pullover at Callum.

'I'm all right,' he said. 'Anyway, it's all damp.'

'Do as Mum says,' Kate told him.

'It's as near as I can get to the school uniform,' said Phoebe.

'It'll stand out, Mum.'

'We'll be gone in a few weeks. Use your head, Callum.'

'Just get on with it,' said Aaron. 'Oh, and Callum ... stand up to 'em. You're a pig-talker's son!'

Callum finished his breakfast; watching his father silently, wondering how Aaron would be when the pig did not come to him.

Phoebe was rubbing her head, muttering, 'I asked you to hang that bacon higher up.'

The day had not started well.

'Couldn't see the pig,' said Kate, who had returned with water.

'Oh, he's there somewhere,' Aaron said.

'I'll come with you, Callum, seeing it's your first day,' said Phoebe.

Turning, he saw his father, half-hidden by the trees, talking to Kate. He wondered: did anyone understand how he felt? Did he understand them, for that matter?

But he was certain of his own feelings: he longed for things to change.

~

Miss Probert said, 'Callum Ward is with us for the rest of the term — or for a few weeks, at least. That's right, Callum, isn't it?'

A few heads turned. Most had seen Callum already. With his short hair and bright eyes and the way he held himself, he looked like a runner — as if his muscles were tightened and he was ready to start. He had taken off his pullover and was seated alone. His hands were tightly clasped, an elbow sticking out of his shirt.

He was getting the feel of the place. He would take all of them on in Computers, Science, English. But he didn't like French much.

'Callum!' Miss Probert was saying for the third time. The class had turned at their desks to look at him.

'You're sitting right in the sun. Surely you're too hot there; why not move up?'

'I'm all right, Miss,' said Callum.

But then the windows were opened because Maurice — who was an undertaker's son — said he was hot even if the new boy wasn't, and then the others agreed.

'Please, Miss, I think they're boiling the pigswill down at Mr Finnegan's today, Miss,' said Maurice, who had known this beforehand.

'I am sure of it,' said Miss Probert, as a rich smell filled the room. 'You'll get used to it in a few minutes.'

'They've boiled up a lot of ostriches because the meat inspector condemned them, I expect, Miss,' said Maurice.

'I can't smell anything much,' said Victoria.

'Now, class, the last time we talked about this, what did we say? Come along ... Victoria has a damaged olfactory nerve. So, Maurice, what part of you do you use when you smell something?'

'My nose, Miss.'

'Your olfactory sense,' said Miss Probert sharply.

'It's just ordinary pigswill,' said Callum in a clear voice.

'Of course it is,' she said, her voice breaking the sudden silence. 'Callum should know.'

'How do you know it is?' asked Maurice.

'Because we're to do with pigs.'

'Yes,' said the teacher a little awkwardly, feeling obliged to come to Callum's aid. 'And Callum and his family are here to help poor Mr Finnegan.'

'I've seen him,' said Maurice. 'They're pitched off the road.' Turning to Callum, he asked, 'You're travellers, aren't you?'

'My dad's a pig-talker,' said Callum, his face going white.

The laughter was brought under control. Callum stared at his persecutor whenever he looked back. At last the lesson was over. As they sat waiting for the next one to begin, it seemed as if he had been forgotten. But then Maurice started grunting. Most of the others — but not Victoria — joined in. They did not turn round.

~

Mostly, the wind blew from the west ... and from Mr Finnegan's. It came over St Bidulph's Primary School first of all; then — having delivered the ripest smell there — over the rest of the village, stiffening the flag on the church, straightening the weathercocks, swinging the sign outside the post office, where they sold tea and soft drinks on tables outside.

Below St Bidulph's, the ground fell away sharply to a cleft which then spread its sides, forming a small valley with one slope half-covered in tin huts and pigs. At the far end of this slope was a small field of corn planted on the previous year's feeding-ground. It was an old-fashioned way of pig farming, and one which Mr Finnegan liked because he believed pigs, too, had a right to happiness.

The other valley-side was wooded. It was high upon

this slope, where the trees grew right up to the lane connecting with the village lower down, that the Ward family had settled.

In the bottom of the valley, with pigs on one side and trees on the other, was Albert Finnegan's cottage. Near it was the boiler house containing Numbers One and Two boilers, and standing by them were a couple of skips for the collection of chicken carcasses, pastry offcuts and the like, and plate-waste from the hospital and several hotels. And then there was a tanker for waste yoghurt and buttermilk from the creamery. Number Two boiler was used for special consignments that needed extra boiling-time on account of their general state and nature. For instance, the ostriches would have gone to Number Two.

When the wind was from the north, coming off the heather and pine woods, there was no sweeter-smelling place than Edgehill, nor a better one — Edgehill, with its quaint cottages, and blackbirds pecking on the lawns, and the sound of the children of St Bidulph's during break carrying over the village into the sky where the gulls cried.

When Finnegan's Wind — as Miss Probert some-times called a westerly — was blowing, and it was cold, the smell was not quite so bad. On a warm day it was smellier. But when the boilers were working, whatever the weather, the smell came over as fearsome. A moist breeze was, perhaps, worst of all. The smell would linger and run in the droplets of water. It would settle on plants, on paintwork, in the fur of cats and dogs and on villagers' fingers, so that there was no one who had not cursed the swill-making in Edgehill; and Albert Finnegan; and the local council for not closing him down.

Albert Finnegan, on the other hand, did not mind the smell.

When an interesting lot of remains had come in and they had been slopped and shovelled into a boiler, and when they had then come to the boil, Albert would stand back and sniff with pleasure. For high-risk material, which was often the smelliest, the heat had to be held at 133°C for twenty minutes. When it cooled down, it made a wonderful wet feed. Then Albert might even try a bit of it on the end of his finger. It was remarkable what boiling did.

Albert enjoyed the smell of the pigs, too. Sometimes it was better than at other times. In the long, hot days with no wind, the sun would heat the pig-dung, and the smell would rise up and hang over the farm. Then, in the evening, the cooled air would slide down the valley-sides and collect around the cottage, with Albert himself probably nodding off in his chair, at peace generally with the world.

His cottage was more like a hovel, with one room up and another in the attic, and one down, and a damp kitchen and bathroom at the back. Around the cottage he had planted a lavender hedge on all sides, broken only by a tumbledown gate to the front door. If the wind was blowing sweetly from the direction of St Bidulph's, he would often bend down to sniff his lavender. If it was blowing the other way he did not bother.

For years, there had been such hostility.

Now it was 'poor Mr Finnegan'. Like Miss Probert had said: 'Callum and his family are here to help poor Mr Finnegan.'

Albert was dying.

Everyone knew it. Maurice — because of his father's interest in it — certainly knew. The postmaster, who

had frequently complained to the local council about
the swill nuisance, had heard about it. He was already
planning to put more tables outside for teas; for most
assuredly, he thought, the piggery would soon be
closed. Miss Finnegan's dislike of her brother's pigs
was well known.

Miss Probert said the smell was probably worse
these days because Mr Finnegan could not manage
all the jobs that had to be done. For instance, when
Albert drove the skips through the village on the way
to collect a load, they smelled as bad empty as they
did when full ... and sometimes worse. And what a
blessing, therefore, the Wards would be.

Albert's sister, Lizzie Finnegan, had been the first one
to know he was dying — apart from Albert himself,
who was of the same opinion, and of course the doctor
who had listened to his heart and said, 'You'll have to
take it a bit easy now, Albert. Can your sister help you?'

'Lizzie? She never did like the smell. That's why she
lives outside the village. Even when she was little she'd
run off into the heather.'

'Could you not give up pigs, then?' the doctor had
asked.

'Never,' Albert said warmly.

'What about the swill?'

'It's part of the job. Pigs need swill. You can't have
one without the other.'

∼

As soon as he met Aaron, Albert had explained: 'It's
gone downhill on account of the state of my health. The
pigs are not happy. Number One boiler needs cleaning

out. Likewise the skips. Chicken innards are not being mixed with enough pie-trimmings.'

'That's bad,' agreed Aaron, ready to give Albert an idea of his knowledge. 'Pigs has got to have just the right balance of protein and carbohydrate.'

'And seeing the corn's been cut, they want to get in the new field.'

'It'll be done in no time at all. My missus helps with fencing, and we've a lad....'

'You must call me Albert,' he said. 'You got a family, then?'

'Boy is coming up twelve and wanting to go his own way already. Girl's sixteen ... finding fault.'

'They often do,' smiled Albert. Then: 'You want to know why I need you? I mean, apart from what I said. I'll tell 'ee. Maybe Lizzie'll sell it as a pig farm after I've gone. Maybe not. I don't know, but I hope so. Don't like the thought of houses being built here. Been a pig farm in my father's time and his father's before that. But most of all, I want you to get it looking good again. You know what I mean ... pigs happy, strong swill. So's I can look at it once more like the way it was before I was took ill.'

Then Albert saw Callum at the door and asked him to come in, and he rested a hand that was light and quivery on his shoulder.

'Where's your missus?'

'Outside.'

'And your daughter? So bring 'em in!'

Then Albert was beaming at them all, but a little lost for words, saying only, 'Well, then, here we are!'

~

Each day after school, Callum worked with the pigs, cleaning out the troughs, inspecting new piglets.

'They're in a state!' said Aaron.

'I've never seen such a sorry lot,' agreed Phoebe.

But already there was the beginning of a new spirit amongst the pigs. It was faint enough for Callum alone to feel it.

It was because he was amongst them.

~

At St Bidulph's, Maurice had quietened down. Also, the boil-ups at Finnegan's had blown the other way. Victoria asked Callum if he could smell the swill like the others, and he truthfully had to say he did; but what did it matter? He liked it!

Miss Probert told him, 'You've a high reading age, Callum. I'd expect it of someone of fourteen, or more ... much more.'

And still his elbow stuck out of his shirt.

A wet wind howled in the trees. Aaron had built an open shelter — nothing more than a tin roof on four posts. There was a hole in the middle to let the smoke escape, although much of it was blown away through the open sides. It was an eating-place for them, more suitable than the hut.

One evening Callum went out to the pigs and told them: '*Look, you know Albert is dying, this I understand; but he is happy! So don't you be unhappy because of it. It is now your purpose in life to be happy for the sake of your master. There is time for you to do this, I promise you, although your own lives are short.*'

He was taken up, in that moment, with the feelings

of the pigs. He looked up at the wrinkled sky and was certain the gulls and crows — and, further on over the moor, the sparrowhawks and the harriers that preyed on the rabbits — also knew about Albert Finnegan. Their sorrow was ending.

All around him the pigs were squealing and snorting.

~

Although Aaron went about his duties on the farm to Albert Finnegan's great satisfaction — for the improvement in the pigs was obvious to everyone — he had lost a great deal of confidence. This was due to the pig that, he thought, had simply gone back to its owner of its own accord.

It was an evening of candlelight in the hut, with Kate looking softer, stroking the mouse, and Phoebe with a needle and a great pile of dresses at her feet, and Aaron spinning his thoughts.

'I've lost my powers with pigs,' he said.

'What nonsense,' said Phoebe. And then, making Callum feel guiltier still: 'It's a gift you've got. There's been such a change in those pigs for the better — can't you see it?'

3

Living near a stream was essential for the Wards. One reason was that Aaron did not feel at home on a new site until he had 'gone piggin',' as he called it. And as the clouds of blood were replaced with clear water, so his guilt, if he felt any — which he occasionally did — also vanished.

If it was clear and sparkling with light, and there were sticklebacks; if it was fast-flowing off the moors and the river-weeds were bright green; and if the wagtails took the water, and the sparrows also — then surely it was good enough for the Wards' washing-water!

Phoebe washed dresses by the water's edge. Then she hung them on a line, ten or more at a time, to rinse in the rain, then to dry. She begged them from the Big

Houses, as she called them. People were glad enough
to get rid of their unwanted ones; and were amused,
perhaps, by the travelling lady with a finely creaking
willow basket full of dried lavender or primroses,
according to the time of year, who then offered them a
bunch in return.

She cut the dresses here and there; she altered and
shaped them. She embroidered and buttoned them and
had a box full of thimbles, some silver, some tin, others
of china. She blew her cheeks out as she remade the
dresses and sewed on buttons, and would not talk to
anyone as she was doing it. She ironed them with a
copper iron, heated on a tin tray that she placed on the
embers of the wood fire. Then she packed them in
boxes and sprinkled them with sweet-smelling herbs.

Three or four times a year, Aaron would take the
dresses to the nearest market and spread them on a
trestle table. Phoebe's earsplitting cries would draw
the people, often to the annoyance of other traders.
Carefully dried and cleaned rabbits' paws were offered
as lucky charms to persuade people to buy, although not
everybody liked them, and some drew away in disgust.

For as long as Callum could remember, his mother
had run such a business. He grew sleepy watching her.
He felt so peaceful he could not tell where his legs
were, except by looking at them. To him it just seemed
natural, something which always went on. It was a pity
that he was no longer proud of it. It was not easy for
him when it got back to him, at school.

Phoebe was buttoning a dress, a thimble at her side.
On the floor at her feet were a few dresses she had
collected during the week.

Aaron turned up one of the lamps and said, 'All
right, then?'

Callum was nearly asleep, his eyes stinging a little from the fumy air, an opened school textbook on his lap. He was thinking this: With information ... it was up to him how he used it. Anything he wanted to know was out there. Also, maybe he would not want to use it.... He lowered down thoughts like these as if they were on pieces of string.

Kate lay on her bed. She had put some torn dresses, ones which were of no use to her mother, in the mouse-box. The lid with the air-holes had been taken off; the box was quite deep enough to prevent the hundred or so mice from jumping out, although it had been necessary to close it on the journey. Knowing they were safe, she gazed at the candlelit icon on the wall, her eyes dancing as the flames waved in a draught.

Also, there was a special mouse, alone in its own cage. It, too, had one of Phoebe's dresses.

Kate often washed the dresses, tipping the colony of mice into a clean box, so the air in the hut smelled sweet enough at most times. But that night it smelled mousier than usual.

Outside, a police car pulled in off the road.

'This is it,' one of the policemen said. 'We'll search under the trees first of all.'

~

Kate had already coaxed the special mouse back into its cage, with the aid of a piece of special cheese. A flap allowed it to go in but not to come out. The colony of mice started squeaking as one, tumbling about in the box and making a great noise, knowing that their food was also to come.

Then there was a knock on the door.

'Keep those mice quiet!' hissed Aaron.

Kate quickly scattered a mixture of meal and ordinary grated cheese in the box, ruffled the dresses and told the mice to be quiet — using the back of her mind, a private place where she could never hear wind nor rain nor music, nor anything else, but only the thoughts of the mice.

Once again there was a knock, and this time a shout: 'Open up. Police!'

As soon as Aaron opened the door, a torch was shone in his face.

'Mr Ward? I'm from the CID,' the constable said, showing his card.

Aaron nodded. 'That's me.'

Phoebe continued with her needlework.

'Interesting little place you have here. You like bacon?' the constable asked, peering between the hams that hung from the ceiling.

'Taken with the right amount of vegetables, it's a healthy diet, yes,' said Phoebe, putting down her needle.

'Pigs are my life,' said Aaron.

'In what way, sir?'

'I help out pig farmers, especially those with troublesome pigs — pigs that don't fatten, pigs that fight amongst themselves, pigs ...'

'Any other interests, sir?'

'As it happens,' said Aaron, beginning to show his annoyance, 'we have.'

'Like this,' said Phoebe, holding up a dress.

'Also, I believe you make mousetraps — not those that kill mice; more like cages, I hear. Is that one of them?' asked the policeman, pointing to the cage where the special mouse was still eating cheese.

'No, it's not,' replied Aaron. Turning to Kate, he said, 'Show the officer one of the traps, Katie.'

'It's humane, the way it works,' said Phoebe. 'You leave it with a nice bit of cheese. Mouse goes in and the door drops.'

'Then what?'

'Then you take it somewhere far away and open the door, and it gets lost, the poor little thing, and doesn't trouble you any more.'

'And you make them?'

'That's right, Officer, and Katie here decorates them.'

'I see,' said the constable. 'Well, don't let me disturb you.' Then, peering between two hams, he asked Aaron bluntly, 'Have you stolen a pig recently?'

'Look at the age of this bacon,' protested Aaron. 'Would you say we've just started salting it?'

'No, I wouldn't,' the constable said, 'and that's what puzzles me.'

'We don't want any trouble,' said Phoebe, re-threading her needle.

'But you had some at your last place. Your caravan was burned down.'

'We didn't make a complaint to the police,' Aaron said. 'How d'you know?'

'It's reputations, sir. You've a reputation, and it follows you. And there was something about a plague of mice, too. You know nothing about plagues of mice, sir?'

Aaron did not answer, for the policeman had started sniffing, moving past a ham, towards Kate and the mouse-smell.

Callum prayed secretly, as a vein throbbed on the side of his head, about the state of the constable's olfactory nerves. It was a fact, Miss Probert had said, that the

longer you were in the midst of a smell, the less likely
you were to notice it.

And, true enough, after a moment, the policeman
said only, 'It's a bit close in here.'

'Anything else?' asked Aaron.

'Just go carefully, sir,' he said. 'Good night, all.'

As soon as the police had left, Phoebe said, 'Just
think what would have happened to you, Aaron, if
that pig hadn't gone. Perhaps you'll cheer up a bit now,
will you?'

'Yes, you've been really miserable about it, Dad,'
said Kate.

'No, I've not.'

'You know you have,' said Phoebe. 'You've lacked
confidence. You should remember that things sometimes happen for the best, though we don't know it at
the time. And I'm certain of this: if it weren't for the
cussedness that took hold of that pig, you'd be up in
front of the magistrate.'

'Yes, all right,' said Aaron.

'Fancy asking us how we earned our money!' said
Phoebe.

'No harm in that, Ma,' said Aaron. 'He seemed to
know, anyway.'

'Why do we do it, Dad?' asked Callum, pressing
so hard on the textbook that the skin on his finger
whitened. 'We're always in trouble.' He asked again,
'Why do we do it?'

'Do it? What do you mean? You listen to me, my
boy: if we don't all do what we're good at and bring in
some money fast for a new caravan, do you know what
will happen? More than likely the Council will put you
in care! Why not be willing? There's your ma with her
dresses; Katie and the mice; and me with pigs....'

'The boy helps where he can,' said Phoebe. 'Be fair.'

'I am,' said Aaron. 'And he's good with the pigs. I just say, be more willing about everything. Look at Katie!'

~

After this, Kate began to complain about Callum doing so much homework.

'It won't get you anywhere, my girl!' said Phoebe.

Before Callum went to bed, Kate often told him of the close friendship she had with the mice — especially with their leader who was kept in the cage, the mouse with the brightest eyes of all — and of the understandings and feelings that rippled between them. She would ask Callum if he believed her or not, and whether he had listened, and then she would pinch his arm for an answer.

The fact was, he wanted nothing to do with mice.

Although the traps brought in more money than looking after pigs, they always brought more trouble. Callum could see that. Yet no one else seemed to want to make a change.

~

The trap-making had started in earnest. To avoid it, Callum studied furiously. At weekends, when he had to help, he often missed the copper nails and hit his fingers with the pin-hammer, such was his annoyance.

Miss Probert had quickly recognised Callum's unusual thirst for knowledge. Not only was his homework of a high standard; he craved to go beyond it. He had been asked to show some of the younger pupils how to use the Internet.

'Have you got a computer at home?' asked Victoria innocently.

Hearing this, Maurice said something about candle-power which made the others laugh. Callum flushed, but didn't answer.

Then Maurice said, 'Your mother's been begging for dresses.'

'It's not begging.'

'What is it, then?'

'It's not begging, all right?' said Callum.

Later there was this, too: someone had seen the police car. Still Callum held his own in class.

For several days Finnegan's Wind had been blowing. The windows were open. And below, there was Callum's father driving Albert's lorry — for all to see — on his way to the chicken factory. The empty skip was smelling as strongly as it ever had. Even Victoria seemed to catch a little of it.

But no one said anything more. They'd had their fun.

~

Kate had washed the mouse-dresses and put the colony of mice in a clean box. Supper was bacon butties. It had been a good day at school, Callum thought, and he had stood up to them. Only one thing bothered him now.

Why, he thought — since he had returned the pig — were the police looking for it?

Unless, of course, he had taken it back to the wrong farm.

4

Albert's valley was often filled with the squealing of his pigs as they enjoyed their new existence, nosing and grubbing in the freshly cut stubble. Albert himself seemed to have gripped on to the bar of life like a man on a trapeze, and to be gliding away from the death that was promised to him. His contented smiles went to Callum's heart. They prospered in each other's presence.

Phoebe stitched dresses, Kate sang songs on her own, and Aaron worked from sunrise to sunset tending the pigs or swill-making.

Miss Probert was impressed with the change in the smell of Finnegan's Wind.

Maurice had been looking out of the window and had seen the steam coming out of Number Two boiler.

He had run his fingers agitatedly around his neck, saying he was hot and pleading for fresh air ... to which Miss Probert agreed, but in a way which did not please him: 'We can't have Maurice suffocating, can we, class?'

And when the window was open, she said, 'And now, Maurice, what is the name of the nerves you are using?'

'I've forgotten, Miss.'

'Victoria?'

'Whatever it is, I haven't got any, Miss.'

'Of course you have, Victoria. They are only a little damaged, that's all,' Miss Probert said. Then, turning to Callum: 'Well, Callum?'

'Olfactory, Miss.'

'That's right. And the smell's so much better, so much nicer,' she said, sniffing again.

'We've hosed out the skips,' said Callum.

Later Miss Probert said, 'Callum, will you help with Michael's reading? Listen to Callum, Michael. You can do it, too.'

Under his breath, Maurice said, 'It's a really weird thing you do — all that with pigs. Everyone thinks so.'

'I don't,' said Victoria.

'You wouldn't, would you, with your nose?' Maurice replied.

After school Victoria said to Callum, 'You could come over, if you want. I live with my mum. Sometimes it's pretty boring.'

~

Boxes full of mousetrap lids — many of them already painted — and mousetrap sides and doors and brass hinges had been brought in from the tarpaulin-covered lorry.

'As soon as it's school holidays, my son,' said Aaron, 'you'll be on this full-time.'

'I know, Dad.'

'In the meantime, he studies,' said Phoebe.

'I don't dispute it, my love,' said Aaron.

'Well, you should, Dad,' Kate said. 'I do all the painting, and Callum only helps to put them together when he can spare the time.'

'Don't contradict your ma,' said Aaron gently.

~

Callum knew it would soon end — the pleasure of being in one place, of making friends. Even Maurice spoke to him ordinarily now, when the others were not listening.

The colony of mice in the box had been taken down to the village and freed. Already they would be mixing with the village mice. And soon — after the plague — the Wards would have to move on. The trick would be to sell all their traps by that time.

It seemed likely to Callum that, by his intervention, he had made pig-stealing a thing of the past. But there was nothing he could do about the mice.

~

'Your ma's got the selling instinct,' said Aaron. 'You can learn selling from her, the same as you can learn about pigs from me.'

It was true enough.

'Nice, aren't they?' Phoebe was saying. 'They don't come cheap at five pound each ... but the work in them! And, apart from doing the job, they're a pleasure to look at.'

'What are they?' asked the village postmaster.

'Little works of art. But mousetraps, really. They capture them. No nasty killing, no mess. I'll appoint you the agent for them round about here.'

'You'll do no such thing.'

'You could start off with six.'

'Why should I do that?'

'To give yourself confidence,' Phoebe explained. 'Then you could go for ten, twenty at a time ... who knows? The more the merrier. We need to sell five hundred of them before it's all over.'

'Before what is?'

Callum, who knew how easily his mother was carried away, and who feared she would answer 'The plague', cleared his throat noisily to bring her to her senses.

The postmaster's wife joined in the conversation. 'Funnily enough, dear,' she said, 'there's been several people have said they've been troubled with mice lately.'

'Look, Missus,' said the postman to Phoebe, 'for a start, most people hereabouts have cats.'

'And they've been acting strangely, I've noticed,' said his wife.

'If they're not up to it — which I doubt — well, then, there's traps that kill, and there's poison.'

'Ugh!' said Phoebe.

'We could try two,' said the postmaster's wife.

'Go on, then,' he replied.

As they left, Phoebe said, 'It's easy. Just don't take "no" for an answer.'

'And it will all lead to a lot of trouble again,' sighed Callum.

'Stop it, now! Your dad's already told you. We get a good plague, a really nice one; then we sell our stock of traps, and, with what we've got saved already, we'll have enough to put down for a new caravan 'ome. What more d'you want?'

'What makes you so sure people will buy them this time?'

'And why not?' said Phoebe. 'Have you forgotten?'

'About what?'

'Their homing instinct. The way the mice'll find their way back from where they've been taken....' Phoebe had started to wheeze as she felt a laughing fit coming on. 'Because,' she continued, 'it's natural for them to go out foraging for their young. So, of course, they've got the instinct to get back ... as long as it's not over water.'

'I know all that, Ma.'

'When the people empty the trap over a wall or somewhere else handy, what do they do? They go and put another piece of cheese in it. And when that little mouse, Callum ... the little mouse ...' Phoebe paused as a fit of laughter finally shook her. 'When the mouse comes back, it has another piece of cheese. Three, four bits of cheese a day ... and it's the same mouse.'

'I know it, Mum,' said Callum wearily.

'It's a carry-on,' said Phoebe, 'and when they tell their friends, "Caught three in one day!" they go out, don't they, and buy one as well.'

~

Within a few days the postmaster ordered two dozen mousetraps. Phoebe helped Callum put them together so that he would have time to do his homework.

She even found time to cook meals for Albert. First she started him on bacon butties with onion and tomato sauce and fresh herbs; and then, when he said he'd never tasted anything so good, she surprised him again the next day with steak-and-kidney pudding, and baked Alaska to follow. And so it went on, and Albert looked better than he had for some time.

Lizzie Finnegan now came in only once a week. She usually made a dish of cabbage, potatoes and corned beef. She sniffed a great deal, as Albert now left most of it on his plate.

Albert, seeing Aaron's state after a day's work with the pigs and the swill — especially after clearing out the boilers and hosing down the skips — insisted again that he should take a bath at his cottage ... daily, if he so wished.

It was then that Lizzie warned Albert, 'They are up to no good — people like that. At this rate, they'll be moving in next!'

But of course Albert would not listen to this. He even invited Callum to do his homework at the kitchen table, which he sometimes did.

Once Albert said to him, 'Have you ever thought of university? You could, a boy like you.'

~

One day after school, Callum finally went to Victoria's house. The walls were lined with books. As he sat eating cake, he thought that Victoria looked skinnier than ever.

Their cat could not come out of the shadows.

'Don't worry, Callum,' said Victoria's mother. 'It's not you. The cat has become very moody lately. There are mice all over the place, and yet she won't go near them; and ordinarily she's such a good mouser. Have you a cat? Do you have the same problems?'

'Callum lives in the wood, Mum.'

'I know,' she said.

So, in spite of knowing he was a traveller's child, she had invited him in! And now she was offering to lend him books — was it not because he had a reputation, a good one, for reading? — and saying, 'If there's anything there that interests you....'

Bitterly he thought that she would know soon. Everyone — including Albert, who had also welcomed him — would know what the Wards were really like.

~

The Wards could have had a steady job with pigs. They could have stayed in one place, living in a cottage with, say, mint by the back door, perhaps rhubarb by the gate, a computer in Callum's bedroom, woodlice on the floor, and nothing changing too much ... had it not been for the mice.

They earned more by starting plagues of mice, and then selling the traps, than from anything else. They had travelled far, trailing their glittering chrome-plated caravan — now a burnt-out wreck — and spending their money on a great variety of pleasures, because of the mice. Then — because their reputation could not get much worse, anyway — Aaron had started pig-stealing.

It was Phoebe who had noticed the fearlessness and intelligence of that first mouse. It was the ancestor of all those special mice that had always multiplied wherever the Wards pulled in their caravan — to their great advantage.

The idea of the traps had not come to her straight away.

She had said to Kate, who was then barely seven, 'Katie, you look after this mouse; it's special!'

So Kate had put one of her mother's discarded dresses in a cage for the mouse, feeding it ordinary cheese, allowing it to come and go as it pleased. She had spoken to it, for even then she had had Aaron's gift with animals.

It was the lambing season. One night she awoke and went out into the moonlight to the fields by the caravan, as if spurred by a dream. She took a bucket and one of the ewes allowed her to take milk, for Kate was gentle, and her understanding of the ewe's situation took the animal quite by surprise.

Kate had asked Phoebe for help to make the first lot of cheese; and the mouse, when he tasted it, spun around in the twigs and cobwebs, nearly mad with delight.

She had said to the mouse in a silvery voice which no one but she and it could hear:

'This is the deal: I will go out into the fields and copses and take milk from the ewes, and I will make cheese, which I will keep safely wrapped in waxed cloth, especially for you.

*And you will come back to your cage every night. And that
way we shall be friends.'*

This had worked very well. Then the special mouse
brought a female in from the woods. She had been
scarred in cat-fights and had survived attacks from
owls. Not only this: she had shivered alone, near to
death from poisoning. She had dreamed near-to-death
dreams of soft hayricks, and of being behind boards
where the dust had never moved since mouse-life
began. Now she had found safety, and she nested with
the special mouse.

Kate had fed that first colony with oatmeal and a
small amount of ordinary cheese, keeping the ewe's-milk
cheese for the special mouse in its own separate cage.

Then Phoebe had thought of the traps. Aaron made
a few, although Kate had not yet started to paint them,
and they profited well from it.

Once, when Callum was ill, Kate had told him something about the mouse. This is how he remembered it:

'The mouse is wounded, Callum. It's going to die.
I'll find the strongest-looking mouse from the colony to
stay with it in its cage.'

Callum had been quite seriously ill then. A doctor
had come to the caravan and the curtains were drawn,
for Callum had measles. Everything seemed to be
disappearing down holes. He heard them talking,
making tea, opening a tin ... but he could not get their
attention.

Kate had come to him again, and said, 'This is a
secret, Callum. Mum doesn't know, nor Dad. The
mouse stole Mum's tin thimble a long time ago. Now
that it knows it's dying, the new mouse will wear the
thimble for an instant, and so it will become the new
mouse-king.'

Later, Callum had once questioned Katie about the story of the thimble. She denied saying it. If it had happened at all for her, it was now a lost vision of her childhood.

～

Phoebe was saying this was going to be the best and most profitable plague of all. She prayed that it would be — for she could put up with the hut no longer!

The colony spread wide in the village. They survived well, all being related to the present leader. Although they had mixed with the village mice, all of them had the genes of that first mouse Phoebe had seen all those years ago. They were fearless of cats. They fixed them with a stare, being blessed with the brightest eyes ever seen in a mouse. On a starry night their eyes would glitter back at the stars.

Of course, cats looked at them. The cats looked, but then they looked away, being uncomfortable. Then they would look again. But the mice still held them with their gaze. The cats felt the power of ages long past, when the Ancient Egyptians worshipped them, wash away through their heads like water.

If some cats still persisted with the idea of killing them, then these mice, who had inherited those quite exceptional genes from their ancestor, simply squeaked. But not as an ordinary mouse would. It was the highest squeak that any mouse anywhere had ever reached. Its frequency hurt. It felt like stones bumping about in the cats' heads.

Some of the mice even attached themselves to cats, as quick as light, and nipped them.

A few — perhaps those who did not have quite enough confidence, or those who in spite of their genes had too easy-going a nature — some were eaten. Some took the poison laid down for them, dying amongst litter and hollows and in between planks and flower-pots, as if by seeking shelter they might live. Of these, a few, though weakened, would return as far as the brook, but, being unable to cross it, would watch the Wards' campfire; and slowly, amongst the raindrops and fallen leaves, they recovered.

They could do it, because of their genes.

~

The leader had gone down to the village. Like a fireball sizzling across the sky, it encouraged the others with its wild bravery, putting fire into their mouse-bellies.

When it returned to the cheese, Kate checked it for wounds.

Of course, Callum could have done it. And he knew about the tin thimble, in which Kate had once believed. He had secretly witnessed at least three coronations. And if he had wanted to be close in thought to the mouse, like Kate, he could have become so without difficulty. It was up to him. He was aware of the mouse's glances; the showing-off of a few high-frequency squeaks.

But he ignored it.

Mice, as far as he was concerned, were no good for the Wards. He longed to be free of them. He dreaded what was going to happen next, after the villagers found out they had been deceived.

But before that, something else happened.

It was in the local paper. A farmer had been arrested for stealing his neighbour's pig, and then released on bail. He said he was innocent. And Callum — who had been uncertain all along about the direction he had taken when returning the pig — knew that he was.

5

Although it was the practice at St Bidulph's for the older pupils to help where it was needed, the head, Mrs Dominic, on seeing Callum with a slow reader in Miss Probert's English class, had spoken quietly with her, glancing once in Callum's direction. When she left, Miss Probert, looking flushed, went to Callum and asked him to return to his desk. She laid her hand on his for an instant.

Callum understood, but not by reasoning. It was like pig-talking, in a way: understanding people's feelings, sometimes whether they wanted you to or not.

Victoria joined him in the playground soon afterwards. Wayne, Darren, Rosetta Briody, Millie Osborne, and the Moynihan brothers — all from his year — and, of course, Maurice with his close friends, were making

a great deal of noise. They often did. Callum was alone
by the fence, looking towards the valley with the sun in
his eyes, catching the occasional sound of Albert's pigs.

Finnegan's Wind was blowing, but not a steady wind,
and it blustered and was uneven and came suddenly;
and with it came the sound of the pigs, and a cloud of
smell from Number Two, which vanished as quickly as
it had appeared.

'You understand what all that was about, don't
you?' Callum said.

'Not really.'

'It's me being a traveller's boy, and the pigs and
everything. The parents don't like it.'

'How do you know that?' Victoria asked.

'I'm sure they don't.'

She shrugged. 'Is that all that's wrong?'

Maurice looked in their direction for a moment,
holding his nose, but Callum ignored him. 'I wish it
was,' he said.

Then he told her about pig-talking, and how it was
not much more than respecting the animal and believing
and emptying your head. And then he told her of the
pig they had taken, and how he had returned it.

'But I took it back to the wrong farm,' he said. 'Now
he's in trouble with the police.'

'He won't be, if you tell them.'

As Callum passed the post office, on his way home,
the postmaster came to the door and called after him,
'Tell your mother to bring some more traps. As many as
she can manage.'

Callum simply waved his hand, without turning.
Outside the village he saw a flock of gulls wheeling up
on thermals in the distance. The wind had changed and
was coming off the moor.

~

Victoria's mother, Mrs Kelly, was impressed with the Wards, and especially with Callum. Here was a boy who lived a quite spectacular life, yet did not appear to know it. His mother's dressmaking would have brought her fame if she had not been a traveller. He had a sister whose strange, heady paintings of flowers persuaded sensible people to pay five pounds for half an hour's work, and a father who had changed the state of the piggery and given Albert a reason for prolonging his life.

Most interesting of all, Callum lived amongst those who, according to Victoria, had a great and unusual understanding of animals.

Neither Mrs Kelly nor Victoria knew what was wrong with their cat. It had become terrified of mice. Mrs Kelly was determined to ask Callum about it, but he had not been persuaded to call at the house again.

There was hardly a single or a widowed lady in the village who did not have a cat. And the nature of all those village cats had altered. Of course, you would expect moods from cats — who could ever truly understand them? But for all the village cats to be affected in the same way.... Something was wrong.

A lot of people started feeling itchy and uncomfortable; looking for mouse-droppings; jumping at sounds under the floorboards; arguing with neighbours.

The sales of traps were phenomenal.

~

Callum's fingers were sore where he had hit them with the pin-hammer.

'Just look what you're doing,' Kate said.

Phoebe was sitting in a corner stitching a dark-red dress, the side of her face shiny with lamplight. Aaron looked up; he, too, was putting traps together.

'We're near the end of them,' he said, looking pleased. 'We've never had anything like it; there's mice everywhere.'

'Maybe Callum didn't wash his hands,' said Phoebe. 'Did you wash your hands, Callum boy? If your 'ammer keeps slipping, maybe it's the fat off the crackling.'

'He likes his crackling,' said Aaron, 'even though we had to buy this lot from the butcher's.'

'I washed,' said Callum.

'Get on with it, then,' said Kate.

It was not an argument. It was often like this. Sometimes it would flare up, but mostly the Wards were simply chattering as they worked: Aaron grunting now and then; an occasional sharp intake of breath, a sigh from Phoebe; the hiss of the lamps — sounds which Callum knew from long ago, and which had stayed the same.

The mouse had been out all day. That night, Kate inspected it for wounds and, seeing none, enticed it into its cage with the special cheese, as usual.

Lying in her bed, she gazed into the mouse's steely bright eyes. She blew out the candle and whispered across to Callum, quite loud, as if she was suddenly unburdening her heart: 'Do you think I don't want things to change, as well?'

~

The next day, Miss Probert was pinning up test results. Maurice bit his lips. Callum's computer studies results were good.

The policeman called in the afternoon. You could see he recognised Callum, but he said nothing.

Miss Probert, after introducing him, said, 'So listen carefully. Most cycling accidents need not happen. And the constable is going to talk about theft, as well.'

After the break, Callum said quietly, 'Please, Miss, I want to speak to the policeman.'

'Then go ahead.'

'Alone, please, Miss,' he said.

~

'It's time to go from here, Ma,' said Aaron. 'I can feel it.'

'Soon, it is,' Phoebe replied, 'but not yet.'

'We've enough money to put down for a caravan.'

'That's nice,' she said, threading a needle.

'What's stopping us going now?' Kate asked. 'Callum's schooling, I suppose? It's all we ever hear!'

'No, not one thing in particular,' Phoebe said. 'For instance, there's also Albert Finnegan.'

'Oh, he'll be all right,' said Aaron. 'Any good pig-man could look after the place now.'

'I doubt that very much,' Phoebe replied. 'Also, there's his health.... He can't cook, and his sister won't, excepting boiled cabbage and potatoes with a bit of tinned meat or something.'

'I see all that, but I can't go piggin' here again,' Aaron said, 'with the police being watchful. And I do miss a dinner of our own pork.'

'You mean, from someone else's pig,' said Callum.

'That will do,' warned Phoebe. 'And you're quite right, Kate,' she continued, 'there is also Callum's schooling. And it's a few more weeks till term is over.'

'Couldn't we go before everyone finds out?' Callum asked.

'Finds out what, dear?'

'You know what I mean: that we're cheats!' said Callum bitterly.

'I didn't hear that, Callum,' said Aaron.

'I did,' said Kate.

'Stop it!' Phoebe said. 'It's always the same. We've got to keep our 'eads. No one's pointed the finger of suspicion at us yet. And in the meantime, we stay put.'

'It's not just piggin'. Look ... I know how you feel about Albert, and Callum's schooling, too,' said Aaron seriously. 'The trouble is our reputation. It's catching us up again. We'll have problems soon.'

'I've not sensed it yet,' said Phoebe.

'It's coming at us from all directions,' said Aaron. 'Last week at the pie factory, there was another pig-man collecting, and he said, "Ain't you the man who took another man's pig and got his caravan burnt down for doing it?" "How could I be?" I said.

'Then, a day later, coming back with ostrich odds and ends, I broke down in the high street of a village that looked familiar. People came out and looked to see what the trouble was, and then shot back indoors quick and closed all the windows. When I'd fixed the engine and was climbing in the cab, a lady came out of her house where a cat was looking out from the curtains and said, "That's him!" "Beg your pardon, madam?" I said. "You're the man with the mice, ain't you?" she said.'

After listening to all this in silence, Phoebe said,

'You should have told me earlier.'

'So it won't be long before we go!' said Kate.

'Why do we do it?' asked Callum, but no one seemed to hear.

~

Callum had become a familiar figure in the village. Because of one or two things Miss Probert had said in the post office, some of the villagers — perfect strangers — now smiled at the traveller boy. They were the old ladies in particular, those who wore lots of clothes in spite of the warm weather and who, as likely as not, had cats in their windows. One of them remarked to another, 'Molly Probert tells me the Ward boy is the brightest pupil she's had. You wouldn't think, with his background ... although maybe it's because of it.' In fact, the villagers seemed impressed with the general industry of the Wards.

More than anything, they had seen the change in Albert Finnegan.

No one liked Finnegan's Wind, because of the swill. They did not mind pigs so much, neither the smell nor the sound of them in that wind. There had always been a piggery, for as long as anyone could remember — in Albert's father's time, and in his grandfather's. Even his great-grandfather had kept pigs.

These days you could not tell whether Albert was dying or not, although he was supposed to be; such was his obvious contentment at the state of his pigs and of Numbers One and Two boilers.

So Callum was given this goodwill too, although it really belonged to his father.

The postmistress said, 'Give this to your mother, will you?' It was another order. 'It helps to keep things regular,' she said.

'Give him some cake,' said the postmaster.

So Callum sat outside at the table in the sun and had a can of fizzy drink, and several people nodded and smiled. They did not notice that his eyes were bright with tears, although the concentration he gave to his drink quickly put an end to them.

He wondered when the police would call.

~

'Can we manage another twenty, dear?' asked Phoebe.

'Just about,' Aaron replied. 'Then we're cleaned out of stock.'

'I expect Callum will be glad, with his poor fingers — won't you, Callum boy?'

Already Kate was packing up boxes.

'We'll be off tomorrow,' said Aaron. 'There's nothing to stop us now.'

Phoebe nodded. 'But it's Albert I feel bad about,' she whispered.

'About the pig,' said Callum. 'It was me. I took it back. Someone else got the blame for stealing it, so I've told the policeman who came to the school.'

~

It took several minutes for it to be fully understood. Callum went over it several times. His throat was dry. At one point, Phoebe was shouting her support for him.

Aaron's anger had left him exhausted.

'One thing's for certain,' he said quietly. 'With the law being interested in us, as you might say, we can't go on the run.'

'So we're not leaving?' Kate said.

'How can we?' Phoebe replied. 'It'd be as good as admitting we're guilty.'

'Aren't we?' Callum said.

The lamps were hissing.

All their faces were set, for a moment, in stone.

6

A storm had been gathering all day, with the clouds packed as close as weeds. And now it rained and the wind hacked at the trees.

'What do we do now, Ma?' asked Aaron, although he had every intention of finding an answer himself in due course. To Callum, his voice sounded layered in between other sounds from the woods. The wind shook the hut, setting all the hams in motion.

Then Aaron lapsed into silence and Phoebe went on stitching her dresses until the storm died down. Kate and Callum then kindled the fire and searched under the dripping trees for wood, and by the time the sun had gone down in a clear sky — and not a word had been said of their troubles — they were sitting round the fire, eating boiled bacon and potatoes followed by hot rice pudding and sultanas.

'What your mother does with food ...' Aaron said, addressing both his children, but then he became lost for words.

'I'm sorry, Dad,' said Callum.

Aaron took his hand.

'I'd do a great deal more if I had an oven and some electrics,' said Phoebe.

'Callum says he's sorry, so everything's all right now, I suppose?' asked Kate.

'No, it's not, and you know it isn't,' Phoebe replied, 'but we've already had an argument. Do you want to start again?'

'All right,' said Kate. 'But let's just talk about it. No, Dad, let me, please. Ever since Callum's been old enough to go to school, he's been excused trap-work except at weekends —'

'In term-time, yes, he has — except this last one, of course, due to the exceptional demand,' Phoebe agreed.

'And what has Callum's schooling done for us or for him,' said Kate, 'except make him do stupid things like returning that pig?'

'To be fair,' said Aaron, 'with the police enquiring like they did, if he hadn't....'

'Miss Probert says that Callum —' Phoebe began.

'I don't care what she says,' said Kate. 'I've had enough.'

'Just listen to us! It's gone very deep, Callum, what you've done,' said Aaron. 'I know you're sorry, my son. But if you'd thought....'

'I did,' said Callum.

'Also, you must have seen me sufferin'; for weeks I was worried I'd lost my powers.'

'Well, you 'aven't, dear,' said Phoebe.

'Of course I'm pleased you've got the gift, Callum boy,' said Aaron.

'I'm not so sure I am,' said Callum.

'It's something to be proud of. Don't belittle your father,' said Phoebe.

'I'm not.'

'Yes, you are,' said Kate.

'One big happy family,' Phoebe said, near to tears.

~

The police car drove through the village. Phoebe was in the back with Callum. As it turned down the track that led to Finnegan's, a couple of villagers turned to look.

They pulled in by the boilers, which had not yet been fired.

'Nice day, gentlemen,' said Albert, leaning heavily on his stick. He had been told what to expect. 'Go right ahead.'

Both policemen seemed greatly amused by the nature of their enquiry.

'It's not as bad as I thought, down here,' said one of them, sniffing.

'Myself, I've always liked it,' said Albert. 'You should smell the boilers!'

'Not today, sir,' said one. 'All right, Callum? Do you want to come, madam?'

'I'll sit here,' said Phoebe. 'Do what the officers say, Callum.'

On the way to the pigs, the policemen asked Callum how he liked school and if he was any good at conkers, but Callum's tongue stuck to the top of his dry mouth.

He got in amongst the pigs and asked one of them to

be good enough to follow him. He lifted the wire to allow the pig through and walked ahead, with tears of anger and perplexity streaming down his face, there amongst the bracken and wild rose and elder that grew on the lower slopes where the wood began. The pig followed behind him, all the way.

When he felt his face was presentable enough, he turned and came back to where the policemen stood. He had left them talking happily to each other, smiling, amused. Now they looked at him with curiosity.

Callum and the officers returned to the car in silence.

~

Callum felt change. It was a definite movement. It took him along like a warm seawater wave. The way things had always been for him was ending.

Albert, strangely enough, had said nothing of the affair — although there had been the opportunity, for Callum studied at the kitchen table now, whenever he could, to escape from the closeness of the hut.

Aaron had been obliged to give a statement to the police, and they had talked with Callum in a separate room, giving him a cup of tea and biscuits. They had warned Aaron to expect a visit from the child welfare department, saying also, 'And, of course, you understand you must not leave the district while further enquiries are being made?'

Aaron nodded.

'Callum's in for it now,' said Phoebe.

'We all are,' said Kate.

'It will be no business of the welfare people's, once we've bought a caravan,' Aaron assured her.

~

The late-summer winds had finished for a while. A couple of trees had fallen near the brook, providing fuel. And although the smell of the drying forest floor was as good as ever, and the fires as red, the magic had gone out of them, and out of everything.

At school, too, Callum felt it had changed for him, for ever. Rumours of the police visit and the pig-walk, which had been seen through binoculars by some villagers, had reached the school.

Callum found that he, too, had changed. Everything that was happening did not affect him the way it had before. For example, Maurice grinned at him in a friendly way for once, and Callum stared back. He ignored Miss Probert's glances of curiosity.

~

The pig farmer Aaron had stolen from had not heard of the Wards before. If he had, it is likely that he would have tried to bring charges, so as to be rid, once and for all, of the nuisance the travellers were causing. As it was, he laughed a great deal at his neighbour's expense. He was the sort of man who kept himself to himself. For him, it was not always easy with pigs; he looked on the serious side. But now here he was, colliding with the furniture and dislodging the dust in his farm office as he shook with mirth. He had been holding it in for years.

But the villagers saw it differently.

It was Aaron's journeys with the skip — especially to the pie factory, where he would meet other pig-men

— that brought the rumours to Edgehill. And hadn't the police called at Albert Finnegan's? By now the postmaster had heard about pig-stealing in other places, and about the mouse-plagues that seemed to follow the Wards everywhere. The story was ready to spread. An hour or so would be enough; then it would be all over the village.

The previous night, Kate had been watched. There she had been in the moonlight. She usually took milk from the ewes on dark nights; now she had grown too bold. It could not have happened at a worse time — these rumours, and sightings.

'Everything considered,' said the postmaster, 'they'd best be gone.'

He kept watch for Callum coming out of school. He had packed up the last few traps.

'Here, boy,' he said, his hand shaking with anger, 'you take these back to your parents. Tell them we've done with it, d'you understand?'

As Callum passed a row of cottages, he saw curtains moving; faces lost in shadows and lines of light on the panes; a fist. A lady came out of one cottage, holding her cat firmly in her arms. She had no front garden. Her doors opened onto the pavement. Callum was close enough to see a collection of hairs on her chin.

She looked straight at Callum, saying to her cat, 'There, don't you mind, my pretty. You'll never understand the wickedness of some people. There's no accounting for it.'

She was very near to shouting at Callum, but she just managed to carry on talking to the cat instead.

~

'There you are, at last,' said Phoebe. 'The police have been.'

'We're free to go, my son. They're not taking it any further.'

'It would have been difficult to bring a charge, anyway,' Phoebe said.

'We'll be gone in a few days, after Albert's found another pig-man.'

'I'll have to take my school-books back,' said Callum.

'You'll have time, my son. Then, with luck, we'll be off before there's any unpleasantness,' said Aaron.

Callum thought: So we'll be on the move again. Then the same old story. Will it ever change?

Phoebe said, 'I'm going down to cook Albert his dinner, no matter what.'

'Can I come, Mum? I could use his table.'

'If it's for study, then yes,' said Phoebe.

'What's the point?' asked Kate impatiently.

'Leave it,' said Aaron.

~

Albert insisted they should both share the meal Phoebe had prepared for him. It was kidneys with fried onion and thick gravy and new potatoes. Callum left much of it on his plate, so strong was his emotion. The window was open. A fine smell of pig and of earth came in, borne by a soft breeze that had stirred through the pines and oaks and ash trees of Mr Finnegan's valley.

'I've already told Aaron,' said Albert, 'that I speak as I find. Never had pigs as happy ... never. And I'll give him a reference, a good one; of course I will.'

'That's kind of you, Albert,' said Phoebe.

'He'll wait until I get another pig-man? Not that he'll be half as good as Aaron. No one could be.'

'He'd better wait, for sure!'

'And I'll miss Callum boy, here, and your cooking.'

Phoebe was biting her lip.

'But if your mind is set on it....' he went on.

Then the door opened and Lizzie Finnegan walked in.

She was shouting at Phoebe. Then at Albert, who had gone white-faced.

Again Callum was overwhelmed by the idea that, because of what was happening now, the way ahead for the Wards had been changed forever.

He hardly heard Lizzie screaming, 'They're evil! Can't you see it? Everyone knows it. Or maybe you haven't heard? There's mice everywhere — and it's them, it's their fault! They're pig-talkers, travellers, thieves, and you don't seem to care. Look at you — you even let them come in and cook you fancy meals....'

'It's more than you did.'

'I've always done my best,' said Lizzie, bringing out her handkerchief.

'No, you haven't,' said Albert simply.

'All right, maybe I haven't,' she shouted, shaking all over. 'No, I haven't! I've hated the pig farm and you in it, year in, year out, stinking the place out!'

'The sooner I'm gone, the better,' said Albert. 'Then it's yours.'

There was silence. Lizzie stood by the window. There were tears of anger on her cheeks. They glistened like glass.

Softly her words came. 'I did not say that,' she said.

~

'The way she went on was terrible,' Phoebe was saying, later.

'How's he taking it?' asked Aaron.

'I'm sure he knows she'd like him to die as soon as possible; then she can do what she wants with the pig farm.'

~

'Enjoy your half-term, Callum,' said Miss Probert, looking doubtful.

'These are my books, Miss. I'm not sure if I'll be back.'

'I'm sorry, Callum, but I'm not surprised.'

'The mice.... You've heard?'

She nodded.

'Me and the pig?'

'But that's good!'

'We shouldn't have took it in the first place.'

'Taken it,' Miss Probert corrected, gently.

'It's what you do that counts, Miss, isn't it? And my pa's set in his ways.'

'What do you mean, Callum?'

'That what happens ... is because of what you've done,' he said, hoping she would understand.

'Not always. But mostly, you're right, Callum. And do something, will you? Don't give up school!'

'I'm not sure, Miss.'

'Wherever you go, school will be a way out for you.'

~

Maurice had heard of the pig-walk.

'That's really cool, Callum, with the pig. How's it done? Could I do it?'

There seemed to be no sign of the old hostility towards Callum; no scorn.

'I don't know. I suppose you could. I don't care,' Callum said.

'We could be friends, you know, if you showed me.'

Victoria had joined Callum. 'I wouldn't listen to that,' she said.

'Then ... p'r'aps we couldn't be friends, after all,' said Maurice. Suddenly he added, 'She's soft on you.'

'No, I'm not. Don't be so stupid.'

'You are,' said Maurice.

'We're going, anyway,' Callum said.

7

Another pig-man had not yet been found. And for as long as the Wards were here, they were looking after Albert.

The thought of him surviving the winter because of their loving care troubled Lizzie Finnegan.

'If he died peacefully, before winter sets in....' she said to the postmistress.

'It would be a happy release for him, dear,' said the postmistress. She knew that, although Lizzie might not actually want her brother to die, she was already looking forward to the advantages it would give her when he did.

'I'd move in now; I'd cook for him ... if it weren't for the Wards. I'd do his washing, keep the fires stoked up....'

'Not the swill-boilers?'

'Drat the boilers!'

'I'm sure you want to help, dear.'

These days, providing Finnegan's Wind was not blowing, Lizzie would often come into Edgehill and stand by the road at the foot of St Bidulph's. She would stare across at the piggery set in its valley. She would purse her small mouth as she thought of the changes she would make. She did not take much notice of the shadowed woods, nor of the birds hanging in the air.

~

The social worker joined the Wards, who were seated round their fire.

'As it's your lifestyle, Mr Ward, we don't want to interfere.'

'Then you're doing it quite well without even trying. What it would be like if you really wanted to interfere, I dread to think,' said Phoebe.

'But we're concerned for the boy in these conditions, Mrs Ward.'

'You wouldn't have even heard of him if it hadn't been for the pig,' said Kate.

Aaron said quite plainly, 'All right; so as soon as it turns really cold, we'll have to buy the caravan. But we can't go yet.'

'You don't have to. No one is asking you to.'

'The hut isn't exactly a valuable piece of property, is it? But if we get a new caravan, it'll be risky keeping it here,' said Aaron. 'They could burn it.'

'Whatever for?'

'Feelings are beginning to run high,' said Phoebe.

The social worker shrugged. 'I take your word for it. So why not go?'

'There'd be no one to look after the pigs,' said Aaron, 'and until another pig-man is found....'

'Pig-man or no pig-man, we're not leaving here, whatever happens to us,' said Phoebe, flushing, 'not with Albert — Mr Finnegan, bless him — in the state that he is.'

~

The leaves were changing colour. And next term, Maurice, the others, Victoria, all would be moving to Middlemoor Secondary School.

Each night the village mice poured out of the darkness.

The Wards remained ready to go. Some packed boxes were put in the lorry, where, Aaron said, they would be safer.

'I wouldn't be so sure,' said Phoebe.

Aaron was avoiding the village each day by walking — often sliding — down through the woods to the piggery.

'We're not criminals, Dad,' said Kate.

Callum roamed the woods for fuel. He crossed the brook to gather wood from an oak fallen many years ago, and worked on this for a whole day, jumping on the rotten branches until they broke.

Towards the end of half-term he called at Victoria's house. Mrs Kelly, seeing his pinched-looking face as he came to the door, let him in immediately.

'Victoria isn't here, but look — I've just made a pot of tea.'

Callum shivered with cold. Then, as quickly, the

feeling passed. He struggled with drowsiness. Drinking, he noticed how much his fingers smelled of wood-smoke.

Meanwhile Phoebe went about her business of looking after Albert; going through the village with her creaky willow basket; catching the bus into town for food. As she waited for the bus, she stared straight ahead, looking at the rooftops. Others, waiting too, clustered around her, staring, open-mouthed, speechless at her cheek — her defiance of them.

~

The mouse was in its cage all day and night now.

'All this waiting,' said Kate. 'It's not natural for it to be there for so long.'

'On no account is it to be let out,' said Aaron.

'It goes mad about the cheese,' Kate said. 'It would always come back.'

'Yes, but when?' Aaron said. 'We could be going any time, and we don't know when.' Then he added, 'Don't forget, that mouse is our livelihood. We must take it with us wherever we go.'

That night, Callum watched the mouse. Kate was lying on her back, her features softened as usual by the candlelight. The eyes of the mouse glittered as he returned Callum's gaze.

Callum thought: *'The fact is, we'd be better off without you and your family! You're destroying us.'*

Kate said quietly, 'You can mouse-talk too, can't you? You've just kept it secret, like you did with pig-talking. You could look after the mouse as easily as I can.... I've thought it for some time now, Callum.'

Callum continued to gaze at the mouse, saying nothing.

'You can understand what it's feeling, can't you?' she asked.

'I don't know. I think I can. It refused to understand what I just said. But I know it wants to get out of here.'

Then the mouse spun around in its cage. It danced and whirred so incessantly that, for a time, the air smelled of mouse-dust and fur. Then it became still and its eyes caught the candlelight again.

'For years I've been doing most of the work with it and its ancestors, so you could do your homework.'

~

Aaron was rarely seen in the village, except when he was driving the skip. It was only the goodwill towards Albert Finnegan himself — in spite of the smells — which prevented an outbreak of violence towards Aaron; for he, driving the skip, was going about Mr Finnegan's business, and not his own.

But there were beginning to be some good feelings for the Wards, too.

Callum had returned to school after half-term, to Miss Probert's pleasure, having explained the reasons for the delay in their departure.

'Mr Finnegan is a fine man,' she said. 'And your family is doing the right thing. Now, Maurice, when Callum's father drives past in the skip, how does your olfactory sense behave?'

'It makes me feel sick, Miss,' said Maurice, looking hard at Callum.

'The swill is a little strong at times,' Miss Probert

said. 'But the pig-smell ... after all these years, I don't mind it at all. How do you account for that, Victoria?'

'Your olfactory nerve is damaged, but not as bad as mine, probably,' said Victoria.

'No, it's not that. When I was away on holiday, there were some pigs.... I was on a walk. I thought: I like that. It reminded me of being here. You see, I'm fond of the village — St Bidulph's, even,' she smiled. 'And smells are bound up with emotions, feelings, memories. Smells are immediately picked up by the olfactory lobe, which is part of the limbic lobe of the brain ... but there's no need to remember that, it's not on the syllabus.'

'It still makes me sick,' said Maurice.

~

Although, when Phoebe went through the village to Albert's every day, she was ignored, the fact is that many of the villagers — those who owned cats — were not so openly hostile any more. For the cats were feeling better. That is, they were beginning to feel confident again.

Most of the mice in Edgehill, having some of the special genes, were good starers, nibblers and squeakers. But now, when confronted by a cat, none of them felt the spirit of battle quite so much, without their leader.

It was caged in the hut day after day, with nothing but Kate's cheese to be thankful for. Although that was, in itself, a considerable pleasure, it was better when taken after a day of cat-battling.

Without their leader, the ordinary mice were losing great numbers as the days and weeks passed. Cats outstared them, as of old. Owls perched on branches with a beakful of mouse, ready to fly off into the soft moonlight. And the mice weakened quickly with poison. They found shadowed places without delay and rested there. Those traps that were still in use — many had been thrown away in anger — were opened now only in the presence of a cat.

The Wards had not been forgiven. But with the cats' peace of mind restored for a while, it seemed that the Wards could at least go about their business, although Aaron preferred to limit his public appearances to the swill-run.

Also working in their favour was the fact that, because of Phoebe's cooking and general care, Albert was looking and feeling better than he had for months — and the villagers were aware of what was being done for him. Once, Albert had been seen cutting his lavender bushes, ready for the spring.

Hot meals — baked potatoes, pork chops, lamb chops, toad-in-the-hole, thick fatty gravy, roast parsnips; and puddings, puddings made with rice, flour, eggs, runny strawberry jam, topped with cream, sprinkled with icing sugar — all of them were prepared regularly and dished out in sensible quantities, so as not to put too great a strain on Albert's digestive and circulatory systems. And they were always shared — because he insisted — by the Wards.

Often the squeals of the pigs carried in the high winds, sounding as if they were suddenly in everyone's back yard. Then they would go quiet again for a while. You never knew when to expect it.

'They're a happy lot,' said Aaron.

Callum knew this: *They are happy to be pigs. The sun is low in a clear sky, just right for them. It's a good time of year. The mash is good. And Albert Finnegan is not going to die yet! They squeal with the joy of life!*

~

Lizzie Finnegan had not been seen since her outburst.

Phoebe met the doctor on one of his regular visits to Albert.

'So you're Mrs Ward,' he said, looking at her with interest. He spoke quietly, for they were standing at the foot of the stairs, and he had just left Albert resting.

'How is he, Doctor?'

'He is a truly happy man, I would say. He lives for his pigs, doesn't he?'

'Oh yes, he certainly does,' said Phoebe.

'And with you looking after him....' The doctor gazed at Phoebe appreciatively. 'It's not only you, mind. He speaks well of the boy — of all your family. I dare say keeping pigs is a lonely occupation.'

'It's the smell,' said Phoebe.

'Quite so.'

'How is he?' she asked again.

'A while ago I would have said it would be tomorrow, maybe. Or next week ... a matter of weeks, anyway. Soon, to be sure. But now, who knows when it will be? In the meantime, he should keep out of the cold winds.'

~

Kate went away for a day on the buses.

When she came back to the hut, she was as quiet as a nested bird. Alone with Callum, she rested her hand on his arm — she had not pinched him for weeks — and said, 'I'm going, Callum.'

'Where to? What do you mean?'

'Only to Middlemoor. I'll get a job there.'

'But why are you going? Do Mum and Dad know?'

'Not yet.'

'For good? They won't like it. They'll miss you.'

'How about you, Callum?'

'I suppose I'll miss you too.'

'It's not far, and I'll visit. I've got to get somewhere on my own. Also, Callum, there's no need for me here, now.'

~

'What about the traps?'

'We're not doing it any more, Dad,' Kate replied.

'Not at the moment, we're not,' he said, 'but we'll move on, one day.'

'Look, Dad,' Kate said, 'with Albert the way he is now, and Mum cooking for him ... he could live for ages! Really, it's the best time to go, if I'm going at all.'

'I wish you weren't, but there it is,' Aaron said, staring at his feet. 'Town life is a big change.'

'I'll be all right, Dad.'

'I can visit,' said Phoebe.

'Of course you can, Mum.'

'If that's what you want,' said Phoebe, hugging her. 'You're not a child any more.'

'I suppose we could sell traps without them being painted the way you did it,' Aaron said. 'We'll have to, won't we?'

'Anyway, we're not moving yet, so don't worry about it,' said Phoebe.

'And who'd make the cheese?' Aaron asked.

'I'll have enough to do,' said Phoebe. 'The next time

we start a plague, it'll have to eat ordinary cheese and like it.'

'But would it come back each night just for ordinary cheese?' Aaron said. 'Generally speaking, Katie, it's a pity that Callum doesn't have your understanding of them — although there's time for him to learn. In the meantime, we'll keep the mouse in his cage for a bit ... in case you come back, Katie dear. Then we'll see.'

~

The mouse was looking intently at Callum.

'Thanks for not saying anything about me mouse-talking, Katie.'

She shrugged.

After a while, she said, 'It's not just that I want a job away from here. There's some special classes I can go to.... It's all fixed up. I haven't told Mum yet.'

Before Callum could speak, she added, 'They're for reading and writing. Then — who knows? — I might put my name down for college.'

8

Callum had wanted things to change, he had wanted space, and there it was — where Kate had once slept. But he turned away as if the sight of it suffocated him.

Phoebe lit the candles by the Virgin. There were no flowers in the holder. Light caught the mouse's eyes as it sat by a lump of ordinary cheese, which it had half-nibbled, then abandoned in disgust.

Phoebe said, 'It's missing her, I do believe.'

They had all seen Kate off on the bus to Castleton. Now the evening air was cold. As Callum went about breaking the kindling wood, mist formed from his breath. He stirred the pieces of wood about in the hot embers. The flame caught and he put on thicker pieces.

He thought: I can do this very well alone. There is

no difference. She was usually just watching me, telling me what to do, anyway.

'There's a bit of Kate's special cheese she left for emergencies,' said Aaron. 'You'd better give that mouse some, Callum. If it goes on like this, it'll starve.'

'It's pining for Kate,' said Phoebe.

'We'll trap a female for it, for company, then,' Aaron replied.

'No, we won't,' Phoebe said. 'And we couldn't free them; they breed at a terrible rate. We're staying here, Aaron, remember?'

'For a while, we are, yes.'

'So the mouse stays on its own. We're in enough trouble as it is.'

The supper lay on Callum's plate. The water from the boiled bacon and potatoes and onion had been thickened with flour and seasoned with herbs. The bacon glistened. A little wood-smoke gusted into their faces.

'Come on, Callum, eat up,' said Phoebe.

'It'll take us time to get used to it,' said Aaron.

'If it's what she wants to do,' said Phoebe, 'then we must be happy for her.'

~

Callum had washed particularly well before going to bed. The smell of bacon and wood-smoke ... how he longed to rid himself of it! The blanket was rough on his skin; the candle glowed within a spidery ball of light.

He was near to sleep. Kate would have blown the candle out; he would have stayed there, warm, the smell of the smoke from the wick playing around the tip of his nose. I'll do it in a minute, Callum said to himself.

The mouse looked at him, its eyes like flint.

Callum whispered, *'This is all your doing. There are so many problems with you. It would have been better for me if you had died.'*

And Callum believed he heard this:

'There would be others ready to take my place. But, of course, you know what the tin thimble is for.'

The candlelight was leaping about as the wick fell in the last of the molten wax.

Callum shook himself. He believed the mouse-talk to be real, and so it became.

He would have liked to say good night to Kate.

Then he saw the mouse was stretched out by the cheese, looking stiff and unnatural. Alarmed, filled with pity, Callum opened the cage and took it in his hand.

The mouse came to, very suddenly, and ran to the sill of the open window. It whirred around at great speed, as was its habit when there was any sort of occasion to celebrate, filling the end part of the hut with a faint, mousy smell. And then it was off into the night.

~

The first thing the mouse did was to bury itself amongst the leaves and old stumps of the forest. It ate seeds and berries and explored and smelled the delicious night-smells, keeping under cover. It felt the dew formed after sundown spread along its flanks.

Then it searched up and down the brook until it found a fallen willow tree, and crossed by it to the other side.

For most of the village mice, there was of course no reason to find a way of crossing the brook, for the hut was no longer their home. Of the original colony, few remained. There had been much mixing with the ordinary mice of the village, although the genetic imprint of the line of special mice was there amongst them too, by now. But without their leader, they lacked spirit.

The mouse rested the next day, taking moisture and food whenever it needed them.

The girl had left. And the mouse-thought — which was more of a feeling, a sensation — of the cheese she had made caused it to tremble the length of its body.

Feelings which it did not understand had come from the boy, especially when they had looked at each other in the candlelight, and these rested in the mouse's head. Deep in its body, in its limbs and on the skin of its feet, it felt the mystery of the boy and girl.... How could one be so unlike the other?

It was feeling strong again as, moment by moment, it worked its way down the slopes to the piggery and to the village. Soon it would be amongst them — the village mice. They, who were constantly being tempted. Cheese — ordinary cheese — was the death of so many!

It was their nature to be particular — to arrange, count, store, worry, go back to make certain of something. They were like this when tracking cheese. But to die for such an inferior cheese, and in a wretched spring-trap!

The mouse knew what it would be like. It, too, had a mouse-brain. This made arrangements, countings and putting-aways and the like, possible. But there was a part of it which, because of its exceptional genes, linked it to the knowledge of how it would be to die — whether in the beak of an owl, or with the flame of poison in its belly, or getting silly with fear of a cat; or perhaps listening to the sound of a spring-trap whistling towards it.

Indeed, the mouse, in its own way, knew even more of what it would be like. It thought about it for a while, as the piggery lay neatly below.

The end of life as a mouse knew it would surely be like a building collapsing. Floor, ceilings, light-fittings, tins of beans, all rasping and roaring; then a dust rising, and a huge scurrying away of woodlice and other insect inhabitants. Then darkness, taking the mouse in its arms.

~

The mouse's presence amongst the village mice, after its absence, was all the more remarkable.

It squeaked songs about cheese — cheese of all kinds. Because it actually had Kate's cheese in mind, it squeaked with great feeling. The village mice thrilled as they listened.

And the cats! The mice now stared back as they had not done for some time — in fact, ever since the special mouse had been imprisoned.

At first the cats were nervy. These mice did not turn away to hide. For they knew this: to turn, to hide, is to die.

They stared. They even squeaked with their high-frequency squeaks, enabled by those unusual genes and by a thrilling desire to live and to fight. Often now, during such encounters, a village mouse would spring and attach itself to the fur of a cat, filling it with terror.

As before, cats kept indoors. Their personalities changed again.

By now the village mice were altogether different. They came out from under the floorboards, to face the cats who had hunted them.

Their leader loved all this. Once or twice it took gorgonzola cheese from a dish, knowing it was safe because of its superior powers of observation. It even rested with those who lay poisoned, counselling them, touching their emerging souls — which they would need in the mouse-halls and palaces of afterlife — with its own feelings of compassion, as best it could.

It had no wish to return to the hut.

~

Each day after school, until it was dark, Callum had to wait by the willow tree which lay across the brook, since this was the way the mouse would be likely to cross back over the water. He carried one of the last morsels of Kate's cheese — now very mildewed — which had been kept for an emergency, although one like this had not been foreseen.

Aaron said, 'You've only got yourself to blame.' Then: 'The mouse has gone, and, with it, part of our future livelihood.'

Phoebe said, 'Without Kate, my love, that doesn't count for much any more, although you don't see it. And meanwhile, with the mouse escaped.... The villagers hate us more than ever; you can feel it.'

On the Friday of that week, Callum returned from school to find the embers of the fire doused with water, the cooking-pot broken, and Phoebe in tears.

On Albert's advice, they moved the hut and the lorry to the yard where the skip was parked.

'It's a bit powerful-smelling there,' Albert said, 'but at least you've got security. In fact, couldn't you buy that caravan now?'

'I'll not do that until we've left the district ... and there's no hurry for that,' Aaron added quickly.

'If it wasn't for me, you'd not be staying. I know that, and I won't forget it, my friend,' said Albert. 'In the meantime, the boy must sleep in the attic room; and you'll all eat with me, I hope? This has gone on long enough for you all!'

~

Callum was struggling against sleep in his new bed. Moonlight from the dormer window shone on the top sheet. For a moment, pig-squeals broke the silence outside.

Everything was changing. Already his class had been taken to Middlemoor Secondary for the day. What had Miss Probert said? 'Don't give up school. Wherever you go, school will be a way out for you.'

But what if they were gypsies after all, and not — as Phoebe had often said — people who had only got into the habit of travelling in order to escape the consequences of what they did for a living?

And sometimes it was true that Callum wanted to move — to leave Albert's, although they could not —

to spin through the countryside in a caravan, to go back to the way things used to be.

But suddenly there was Kate, in his close-to-dreaming thoughts. She was reassuring him. His olfactory sense played tricks; for, quite distinctly, as if this was really happening, there was the smell of her hair as she turned and smiled at him, her reading and writing books propped proudly in front of her.

9

During the last days of term, Callum seemed to think only of the mouse.

After school, with his pockets full of conkers, he continued the vigil as Aaron had ordered. He walked up the lane, crossing the now-empty site in the woods, then to the brook. He stepped over this by holding on to the branches of a fallen tree.

He waited, quite still, hoping to catch the small sounds of the mouse above the rustle of leaves. He knew that, if the mouse returned, it would do so this way.

The special cheese was in an open matchbox, beside him. Earlier he had taken it to school. He had allowed Maurice to sniff it, and then had watched him with contempt as he staggered away, making so much fuss that Callum was told off by Miss Probert.

'Pigs are Mr Finnegan's livelihood, Callum,' she had said. 'I find the smells quite forgivable, therefore. But to bring that to school....'

After school he had sat alone on the village green with the opened box, so that its smell would be taken into the wind. But although he forlornly hoped otherwise, Callum knew that even the mouse, with its exquisite sense of smell, would not easily recognise the scent of the cheese amongst the smell of pig and the smells of boiled pie-trimmings and other odds and ends.

Phoebe had already spoken with Aaron.

'The boy is filled with guilt. He waits by the brook every evening. He walks the lanes carrying the matchbox of cheese.'

'It will do him no harm,' Aaron had said.

But it was.

Callum spoke this into the wind, which had changed its direction and was now Finnegan's Wind:

'Look, I've known about the tin thimble for ages. I've always had quite friendly feelings towards all your ancestors — and now especially towards you — which I never showed. I do not want you to die without knowing this, although — yes — it would be better if you then were finally gone. But before you die in a spring-trap or some other way, I want to mouse-talk with you once more.'

Callum realised this was not particularly caring, the way he said it, but it was the best he could do.

He left the box in a special place deep in the woods. He thought the mouse might go to it alone, and be reminded of the cheese — and then return home for more.

~

The next evening he saw the mouse lying by the match-box, as if it had been unable to quite reach it, with blood on its back. The mouse watched him and its grey eyes filmed over with loneliness; they were the eyes of a creature near to death. With a cry, Callum picked it up and broke a morsel of cheese in the palm of his hand, and watched the mouse's body quiver in response.

As quickly as possible, Callum took it home. He put it in the cage, making sure there was a thimble in it.

Aaron said, 'My son, if this mouse lives, things will go better for us, and our future will be secure again.'

Callum was immediately sent to the woods with one of their own traps, in which he put a piece of Kate's cheese. And later, having captured a fine-looking male mouse with brighter-than-usual eyes, he put it with the injured mouse so that, if it died, the new mouse could take over from it.

Then Phoebe took these from the hedgerows, the road verges and the fields: yarrow, for stanching wounds; wormwood, for a tonic; butterbur, to bring down fevers; and seeds from the blessed thistle (*cnicus benedictus*) to give the mouse supernatural powers. People in the Middle Ages, at least, had thought this was true; and if it was, Phoebe reasoned, the mouse would need those powers to tread carefully when returning back over the bridge of death.

She applied these mixtures and ointments. Her fingers shook with anxiety.

'You poor thing!' she said.

And Callum mouse-talked, '*I am glad, for your sake, that you have recovered,*' and was aware of the mouse's feelings of polite appreciation in return.

After a few days, the mouse ate some more cheese. Callum took the young male out of the box and set him free over the brook, for a successor was no longer needed.

Callum had not been as affectionate to the mouse as he had earlier imagined he would be.

The fact is that — in spite of his better feelings — he wished it gone again out of their lives, this time for ever.

~

With the mouse back in captivity, the cats had once again started to recover, finding the village mice easier prey on their own. The spring-traps were popular places of residence, as before, and the young owls were putting on weight. As for the poisoned mice, there were so many of them that, if their last dreams could have been stitched together to make a cloth, it would have stretched round the Earth.

~

At about this time, Albert moved his computer to Callum's attic room.

'Everything about my pigs is stored here, Callum: prices, regulations, diseases ... boring! But there are games, too. You can use it.'

'Can you get on the Internet?'

'Not yet. But I'm going to buy a modem.'

Albert's hand rested for a moment on his heart. He added, 'As soon as I can get into town.'

~

Regardless of how the plague of mice was going — up one day, down the next — the fact remained that the villagers were sick and tired of the Wards.

Yet there was no more hostility towards Callum at school. It was almost as if there was no room to spare for it. Maurice — all of them, in fact — were more concerned with the ending of term and the great shift in their lives. They were about to be drawn, with the strength of a tide, into a new order at the school in Middlemoor, whether they liked it or not. Things were going to change.

Maurice would no longer be the most noticeable boy in school. His friends had already spotted his new feelings of insecurity.

'Your dad's always been an undertaker, Maurice?'

'Are you going to be one?'

'D'you need a degree?'

'What's up with you lot?' he asked.

They had become tired of teasing Callum. They were leaving him alone.

But for the villagers there was no getting used to the Wards. They were in league with pigs, with mice! Now they were even persuading Albert to give them shelter!

The villagers hated the scratchings, the nibbling noises, the spoiling of their cheeses. Of course, they could spare a little cheddar for the spring-traps. They liked doing it. But they got wild when they had left a bit of Camembert out by mistake.

Because of the Wards, they were even arguing amongst themselves.

~

Aaron had run a cable from the boiler room to the hut. The hams had been put in the cottage. The strong light changed the appearance of all that was left — and really, with the hams gone, there was very little. Callum was standing by the hut door. Who were the Wards? he asked himself. What little had they done?

Aaron was sitting with Phoebe where Callum's and Kate's beds had been, his hands tightly clasped. Phoebe was thinner in the cheeks. The strain was showing in their bodies, in their faces and in the way they held themselves.

'I wish you had beds, too,' said Callum; 'inside, I mean.'

'There's nothing wrong with it here,' said Aaron shortly. 'Bit smelly, that's all.'

'It's not so bad as it was. After a while you can't smell it quite so much,' Phoebe said.

'Miss Probert says that's to do with the olfactory lobe being part of the limbic lobe. After a while, your brain —'

'What's the use of it?' Aaron implored. 'Knowing something like that ... what's the good?'

'I don't know, Dad. Good night,' said Callum quietly. 'Good night, Mum.'

~

It was not far to the cottage. Here, deep in the valley, one side was quite black with trees; on the other, the pig-huts caught what little moonlight there was. Beyond, where the valley-sides began widening out to the moor, the stars were cupped between them like boat-lights in a harbour.

The door of the cottage was open. Callum could make out the hams on the beam, and Albert sitting by the fire. There were noises as thin as stalks; movements from the wood. Above this was a pig-sound of gruntings and snufflings, and a pig-presence of great, round thoughts of welcome.

It was like this for a moment only — while he believed it to be. Then he was inside and Albert was saying, 'There's no reason why your mum and dad can't stay here for a bit — as long as they want — after meals. It's a pity there's not room to sleep.'

'They don't mind, Mr Finnegan.'

'Pigswill ... the smell doesn't bother them?'

'Not after a while.'

'When it blows from the west, do you know what they call it?'

'Finnegan's Wind,' said Callum.

'Now listen, Callum. Before you go off to bed, I've something to say to you. There's another kind of wind.

'It happens only in the evening, when it's been a warm day. The cooling air slides down the valley, carrying the day's pig-smell with it.

'Remember that, Callum. It's important.'

~

Matters were settled very quickly the next day.

Phoebe said, 'Callum, the mouse is pining again. It will be dead soon, all cooped up, if we don't do something.'

'And we can't let it go again,' said Aaron, 'seeing the state the villagers are in. Both ways, we're beaten.'

'There was always such a bond between it and Kate,' sighed Phoebe.

'It was only the cheese, Mum.'

'It wasn't just that. She would do with mice what your father —'

'Whatever it was, the mouse needed her,' Aaron interrupted. 'Tell her to keep it for us until we move.'

'How can I, Dad? She's not here!'

'What we both thought, your dad and I, Callum boy, was that you could take the mouse in its cage to Castleton, so's Katie can keep it for us, all right? We'll see you on the bus. You're quite old enough now to make the journey, and you'll be met at the other end, of course.'

'But why me, Mum?'

'If your ma goes, Katie may not agree with her. But if you tell her what's been decided ... that'll be that, won't it, my son?'

'Besides, it's all agreed,' said Phoebe. 'I've been to the phone box this morning; Katie wasn't in, but I spoke to her landlady. She's going to make sure Katie's there to meet you. Also, she says she can put you up for a couple of days. You'd like that, wouldn't you?'

'It'll be a change, I suppose,' said Callum. 'But Katie won't like it.'

'She'll like seeing you,' said Phoebe.

'I mean about the mouse — keeping it for us. She's started a new life, Mum!'

But he was not understood.

10

Callum put the mouse on the bus seat beside him, covering the cage with a cloth, for in darkness there was supposed to be peace of mind. He did not imagine it would be so for all living creatures, and certainly it was not for him; he always kept the night-candle alight as long as he could, so that he really never saw much of darkness with his eyes open. The mouse did not seem to like it much, either. Already it had whirred under the cloth, but not as vigorously as before, due to its present weakness.

'Here's your pyjamas and toothbrush, and something to eat,' said Phoebe, handing Callum a carrier bag. Turning to the driver, she said, 'He's being met at Castleton.'

'He's all right, then,' the driver said, having looked

at Callum, and then nodded at Phoebe.

Soon Edgehill was gone, and Phoebe's face lit with smiles was gone, too. The hills and valleys fell away, darkening in the distance, and Callum could not see where their own valley was, amongst them.

~

All the way to Middlemoor, Callum could have sung with joy at the change: the mouse was being taken away, out of their lives ... until they moved again, at any rate. And who was to know how long Albert might live?

It was extraordinary — and foolish, he thought — how much trouble they were taking to keep the mouse alive, so that one day they could breed from it again.

It bothered Callum so much that he had often imagined ways of killing it. It was not like killing a pig, which, he supposed, you could do with a clear conscience, providing it was done properly and without deceit. The mouse he could have killed many times before. By dropping a rock on its cage, for instance. Or, when it had been wounded, by just leaving it. It would be sensible to be rid of it; but in his heart he knew he could not do it this way.

The anger and distress of his parents would be unimaginable. Also, because of the mouse's extraordinary character, because of its genetic imprint, he could not kill it like his father had killed pigs. And, for mice, death came rightly from owls, and cats, and hawks, and other dangers like the spring-trap; this was the natural law. Pigs were different. For a start, they had no predators. For the mouse, the course ahead of it had been set by nature.

He broke a fragment of cheese — to which the mouse, by force of habit, had become accustomed — and pushed it through the bars. Then he ate the biscuits Phoebe had given him. The smell of the chocolate coating lingered on his fingers until they had passed Middlemoor.

At last, in Castleton, there was Kate waving at him, wearing a new coat and looking thinner, but smiling and holding out her arms to him as she never had before.

Her expression changed when she saw the cloth-covered cage.

'Callum, exactly what is that?'

~

'It's mainly Dad,' Callum was saying. They were sitting in a café. It could not have been worse.

'How dared they!' Kate was saying for the tenth time. 'And I work every day.... How could I, anyway? In the evenings I study, Callum. Things you learned ages ago.'

Callum nodded. 'Perhaps your landlady will look after it?'

'She might. I don't know. Look, Callum, the life when the mouse meant a lot to me ... it's all over,' she said.

'For me, too,' he replied.

'I suppose I'll have to look after it ... but only for a short while, tell them. And I don't want to see it just now,' said Kate, as they got up to leave.

At that precise moment Callum felt a movement in the cage — no more than a flutter — where the mouse had spun a little, then rested again in the near-darkness.

~

They walked the narrow streets. The doors of the terraced houses opened onto the pavement. As far as Callum could see, rows of chimney-pots stood out against the city sky. Cats sat at front-room windows.

'Just imagine,' said Kate, 'letting the mouse loose here.'

'Perhaps you could do it,' said Callum.

'Mum and Dad would never forgive me.'

~

'So you're Callum,' said Kate's landlady.

Then it happened quickly.

Callum's olfactory sense was tuning in to the smell of gravy and onion. The landlady said, 'Come upstairs. I'll show you your room. A couple of days will be fine.'

The cloth fell off the cage.

'What's that?' she asked, bending down. A moment later she straightened up and let out a scream.

The cage was put in the back yard.

'I'm not having that in the house, and it won't do out there, either. I'm sorry, dear, but I hate 'em and I can't help it. If your brother wants to stay as arranged, he's welcome, but the mouse isn't — inside, or out there.'

'Then that settles it, Callum. You'll have to take it back. There's a bus, if we go now.'

~

Kate saw Callum onto the Edgehill bus.

'I'll explain to Mum,' he said.

'I suppose it's all right?' Kate said, lifting a corner of the cloth. 'Come and see me again....'

'Katie, what am I to do?'

~

As the bus left Castleton for Middlemoor and home, Callum's spirit was as low as it had ever been.

It was often when Callum felt low, like this, that he could talk with pigs and mice — even, at moments, with trees. It had been mainly pig-talk. It was then, more than at any other time, that the true feelings of one could be exchanged with the other.

The feelings of the mouse came to Callum.

Weakness had left the mouse. It had called on the strength of its forefathers. It blazed with anger. Its genetic structure was safe, intact, together. It had rested in the shade of the cloth, eating more cheese than it had for days.

'*I have been rejected by the girl I pined for. Give me space. I will not leave you.*'

Callum thought privately: I cannot take the mouse home. It is all over, now, whatever Mum and Dad say. Sooner or later, they will forgive me. If I get off at Middlemoor, I can catch a later bus. But if I leave the mouse just anywhere there, it will find its way back to Edgehill, since that is within its reach. So I will have to leave it somewhere where it wants to stay, in spite of its feelings of friendship towards me.

Callum made certain none of these thoughts were

shared with the mouse. His happiness — his whole life, as he saw it then — depended on it.

When the bus pulled into the square in Middlemoor, Callum stepped down, clutching the cage in one hand and the plastic bag with his pyjamas and toothbrush in the other.

The next bus for Edgehill was scheduled to leave Middlemoor in an hour. Time enough to lose the mouse. This was what he had to do, and the moment for it had come.

Callum bought as much strong cheddar as he could with his remaining money, then set about finding somewhere with plenty of drains, loose weather-boarding, and holes or broken windows — an empty old building, of which there were several, where the air was still and pleasant for a mouse. He found an old brewery down a side-street, with a door broken off its hinges. The gap was wide enough for Callum to put the cage inside and the lump of cheese beside it.

He longed to be rid of the mouse. He opened the cage. Inside the great floor heaved off into the dark-ness, and Callum turned and left. He did not bother to take the cage.

There was enough cheese for two, maybe three weeks, giving the mouse a good start in its new life.

He guessed what would happen. The mouse's genes would spread to the ordinary mice of Middlemoor. There would be depressed cats everywhere; pest-control officers; cans of poison; spring-traps; and finally the end of the mouse. And with no thimble, there would be no passing of the crown, no coronation.... It would be the end, once and for all, of the line of special mice!

Callum nearly leapt for joy.

~

He did not know the mouse's heart had also been full of joy — not only at the suddenness of liberty and the sight of great spaces and the shapes which loomed from every corner, but also at the boy's understanding, at last, that captivity was no longer necessary. For it seemed to the mouse that the boy had understood this: because of its loyalty and affection — which it had once felt for Kate — they would not be separated from each other again.

At the bus stop, Callum found the mouse nestling in his pyjamas. Trembling with anger, he returned to the empty building and put the cheese in the carrier bag.

Again, he was careful to keep his thoughts to himself.

~

He started walking to the outskirts of town, having enquired as to the quickest way to the moor which surrounded it.

On the edge of town the skies widened, and in front of him was the moor. There would be water there, and he would take the mouse over it. Callum would find it — this water, wherever it ran; of this he was sure. He would leave the cheese with the mouse. Perhaps also his pyjamas, which he could say he had left on the bus. Callum imagined the mouse finding a new place for living, in the heather. Then the hawks finding it.

For Callum, it would indeed be the final riddance.

So he left the road, which was little more than a

track, in order to find the water. The wind sang in the heather. Several times he stumbled and fell on the rock-strewn ground. The mouse-squeaks coming from his pocket filled his head in a strange way, for there were no other sounds, save for the wind in the heather, and it was as if the mouse had taken over the world.

He had no sense of danger yet. He was so intent on finding a moorland stream of sorts, so that he could also find a new beginning, that he paid no attention to direction. He had not kept the sun to his left, nor to his right, nor noted a particular thornbush or a dip in the ground or a sudden rise. And if he had, it would have made little difference; for it seemed to him that everywhere looked the same.

His common sense told him that if he climbed to the top of the nearest slope, he would see the town. But he only saw other slopes. From one place there was a fine view; in the distance a flock of seagulls appeared and disappeared as the light shone on their white bodies tilting to the sun.

It was then, after the shock of seeing the wild moor ahead of him, that Callum started to scramble. There was still plenty of light. He almost cried out at his own folly in leaving the track. Again he climbed, but whether he was going towards or still further away from Middlemoor he could not tell.

Then he saw a pathway going down to a hollow in the ground, quite far below him, with thornbushes on either side, and a patch of grass in the fertile soil at the very bottom. A rough-looking horse was tethered there, next to a gypsy caravan. Light from the low sun streamed across the dip, so that it looked darker than it really was.

He was so relieved to see signs of life that he had no

fear of who it might be in such a strange place — only relief that he would find his way back to Middlemoor. All thought of abandoning the mouse was set aside — for the moment, at any rate.

~

Gulls and crows were coming in over Edgehill to roost. Many had been feeding on the waste-tips outside Middlemoor; others had been following the plough. High over the moor, a plane gleamed before being lost in the gathering darkness.

In Edgehill, it was like this:

Scarcely a sound was coming from the pigs. Most were in their huts.

There was one star in the sky — there was still much too much light for the others to show. It was Venus, the evening star.

Albert Finnegan had died. It was as if everything, all manner of creatures, knew about it. It was a little early for the village mice to be out, but they, too, seemed to be in no hurry to start their night's foraging.

Even — by coincidence, of course — the fire under Number Two boiler had gone out.

11

She was grey-haired, and bonier-looking than any lady Callum had seen, except once perhaps at the seaside. Her skin was lined with extreme age.

'Hello, little brother.'

There was a tugging of the wind in amongst the heather all over the moor. And there was no sound above this, except for the occasional whistling of the horse's breath and the noise of it pulling the grass as it fed.

'I'm lost, Miss.'

She was sitting on the caravan steps. At her side was a neat pile of cleft willow sticks, kept in pairs with elastic bands.

'They're pegs,' she said. 'Clothes-pegs. Used to be able to get them anywhere. Not any more, my dear; a thing of the past. What's your name?' she asked, looking at him swiftly with bright eyes.

'Callum.'

She carried on cutting one end of each stick, curving each side from the centre and re-banding them. The knuckles on both of her hands were badly swollen.

'Next stage is to wind a strip of tin at the other end; nail it, and there it is.'

'Is it what you do?'

'It's exercise for my hands. I've got arthritis. In my legs, too.'

'I'm sorry,' said Callum.

'No need to be. The pegging buys me food, and hay for the horse in winter. I've enough money put by to go to Spain if I wanted. Funny place to be lost,' she said in the same breath.

'I want to get back to Middlemoor.'

'I dare say you do, but it's not up there; that way's only to Barrow Farm,' she said, pointing to the track ahead. 'You'd have no business there. There's just a lady, old like me, keeps goats. She's never had a visitor as long as I've been here, 'cepting me and the Calor-gas man and him that comes to collect the milk. Keeps cats, as well.'

'Then this is the way back to Middlemoor?' asked Callum politely, pointing in the other direction.

'What are you doing getting lost on a moor, a boy of your age?' she answered.

'It's a long story, Miss. I've a mouse in my pocket — look.'

'So you have, and he's a nice little fellow, too.'

'How long will it take to get to Middlemoor?'

'Takes me nearly an hour, but it'll be half that with your young legs,' she replied. 'And there's no time to linger, with the sun going down soon.'

'I'd better go, then.'

'So you had,' she replied. 'Fancy living here and not understanding the moor a bit better. Whatever path you took, you should have stayed on it.'

'I don't,' Callum said; 'don't live here, I mean. I want to get back for the bus to Edgehill.'

'There isn't one, I can tell you that. There's not a bus goes anywhere out of Middlemoor at this hour. Yes, and you can look worried. So I'd be,' she said, glancing at him. 'And what about your parents, then? They'll be out of their minds because of your foolishness.'

'I left the track.'

'You shouldn't have,' she said, 'but it passes near here; it's not far if you know where you're going. Then we'll go to the police.'

'How will you get back?' asked Callum.

'Oh, I'll get a taxi, although they don't like coming out here, especially at night, the track being rough as it is.'

'I'm sorry, Miss.'

'So you should be.'

'But they won't be worried. My parents won't be worried,' he said.

'Why not?'

'They're not expecting me. No one is.'

The woman looked at Callum's drawn face.

'I'll put the kettle on. You'd best come in, little brother, and tell me about it. Watch the pegs! And I don't want the mouse loose in here, either.'

'Don't worry, Miss. It won't leave me ... that's part of the trouble.'

'So you've lied to your sister, telling her you were going straight home; all right, and so have I lied before when I thought it suited me to do so, although in the end it never did. But for you to lie, and now to get yourself in this mess, just to get rid of the mouse ... when all you had to do was give it poison!'

'I'd never do that,' said Callum. 'I've thought about it, and other ways, a lot, but I couldn't do it.'

'I can see that,' she said, looking at him. 'You must tell me more, for I'm blessed if I understand it ... to go wandering in search of a stream on the moors, when it's so uncertain underfoot all around here — to expose yourself to great danger, just so the mouse can't follow you any more. People can die on the moors, you know. When it's cold, they can. What if I hadn't been here?'

'Sooner or later I'd have seen the lights of the town,' said Callum.

'Yes, when it was dark, I suppose? So you'd have gone straight back, knowing how to miss the bogs and marshy places? There's one place near here, a man sank up to his chest; yelled his head off.'

'I had to try and do it, that's all.'

'What is it about this mouse that makes you so foolish?'

~

When he had finished, he added miserably, 'Everywhere we go, it's the same!'

'By the sound of it, you're not gypsies. Now, I am. Delaney's a fine old gypsy name, and so is Ward, but you ain't one. There's plenty of Wards ain't gypsies. But travellers or gypsies, there's thieves among us as much as among any other people, even the rich and titled. But no good comes of it in the end. And there's nothing been thieved here,' she said, sweeping her hand around the caravan.

'Dad never thought it was stealing, since the pigs would always follow him.'

'Then perhaps it wasn't. Not quite,' Mrs Delaney said. 'But causing plagues of mice is another matter. It's deceiving people — hundreds of them, from what you tell me; getting them to buy your traps, which are no good if you don't understand about mice and all that about having to take them over water.'

'Or two miles away — that would do it.'

'No one in their right mind would go to the trouble, when all they've got to do is buy a nice old spring-trap at a fraction of the price.'

'My mum always said you could rely on people's soft-heartedness.'

'Look who's talking.'

'The pigs we got to follow us ... they were deceived, too,' said Callum.

'If you all like bacon so much, couldn't your dad have got a pig cheap, seeing he works with them?'

'It was a challenge, I suppose,' said Callum.

Mrs Delaney shrugged. 'But with the mouse-plague, you'd bring down a whole lot of people's anger on you. How would an ordinary person know about putting a mouse over water? They must have driven 'em crazy. There's no sound I hate worse than a mouse rattling around in the place. All that nibbling and scratching! And these weren't ordinary ones, judging by the little fellow in your pocket.'

'Wherever we go, it's the same,' said Callum. 'We start off with a good reputation. Everything is fine.

Mum alters dresses. People love it. And the pigs put on weight. And there's me at school and Dad a pig-talker.'

'You like school, Callum? My boy went to school and was clever like you, and now he's with computers.'

'What does he do?'

'I don't know exactly. But he's got a degree, has my boy. Says I need a mobile phone. And so I do. Having one would help me to get you out of this mess.'

There was a silence.

Mrs Delaney stretched a hand, lumpy with arthritis, towards him.

'Everything goes wrong,' whispered Callum. 'It's the mice!'

'So you set about changing things, little brother? And yet you won't drop a rock on it? I'd spill its brains out, little brother, good and quick.'

'Even if I could, it wouldn't be any good. It would know, and move in a flash,' Callum said.

'There's other ways ... and a white cat would be one of them, if it's a natural death you want for it.'

'It can outstare any cat, whatever its colour,' Callum replied.

'I know cats don't like their victims a-staring back.'

'And you should see its eyes when it's cornered,' said Callum.

'I dare say.'

'And it squeaks so high the cats can't stand it,' said Callum. 'I think it's the squeak that puts them off more than anything else.'

'Exactly,' said Mrs Delaney, 'and most white cats, especially those with blue eyes, are deaf. Ask anyone — or a vet, at least. Those cats aren't common, mind.'

'I've never even seen one.'

'There's a white cat lives on the moor near Barrow

Farm. The old lady there had two of them. One died. This one turned wild.'

'It's something in their genes, I expect?'

'They can't hear a thing. So your mouse would be finished off in no time at all. But, mind you, there's other ways,' said Mrs Delaney. 'Like sparrowhawks. They'd find it, sooner or later.'

'I know that,' said Callum.

'It's going to die one day, that's for sure.'

'At least there's no thimble,' said Callum.

'What's the good of a thimble?'

'Without another mouse to take over, not much good,' he replied.

'Tell me about it, little brother.'

Mrs Delaney got up without interrupting and set about lighting the gas lights. The copper and silver ornaments gleamed, and the polished oakwood as well. Callum explained about the coronations that Kate had once believed in, and how they were an essential part of passing the special genes from one mouse to another; and how, when it was crowned, the chosen mouse became even more exceptional due to being and feeling important.

'If it dies, that's the end of it?' Mrs Delaney asked.

'Without a new leader — yes.'

She did not answer, but Callum felt the warmth of the smile in her eyes.

Then he told her about his mother's dressmaking, and how this had been done in the caravan they had once owned — which, although not built in the Romany style like Mrs Delaney's, had had heat and light and Calor gas. He mentioned Phoebe's longing for electricity.

'It's understandable,' said Mrs Delaney.

He told her about the hut. The smells. The hams. Phoebe, regardless of the poor light — the hams blocked out quite a bit of it — using her needle, holding the material close to her eyes. He told her about the great soft moon that so often hung in the mist.

He explained how it was for him when he talked to pigs, and to the mouse sometimes. Then he spoke a little of Kate — whom he called Katie, now — and of his parents, and the hammering he did, and the trap-making.

At that, Mrs Delaney pointed to the pile of pegs lying cleft and shaped.

'Let's see you nail the strips of tin. I'll show you.'

Callum took the light pin-hammer, which was like his own, in his hand; and he knocked the nails in, one after the other, into peg after peg, at great speed, and with never a stroke wasted. He cut the tin neatly off each peg when it was finished, as he had been shown.

'What is it you most wish to change, little brother?'

~

'The fact remains,' Mrs Delaney said uncertainly, 'I should still take you to the police, although I've left it late.'

'I can find my own way.'

'I'm not so sure you can, and I'll not let you try. But my legs are paining me tonight. Besides, there's a change in the weather, mark my words.'

'Also, I'm not expected.'

'I know, and because of that — I wouldn't dream of it otherwise — you can stay here tonight. But I'm taking you to the police in the morning.'

'What about your legs?'

'I'm all right if I don't hurry. Nice and steady, there's no pain to speak of. Now then,' she added, 'my bed is behind that door. I'll put you up here. I've a grandson stays. Tells me things I've never heard of. He's got a laptop computer.

'And don't be troubled,' she said, putting her hand on Callum's shoulder.

After the bedding was in place, she added, 'Now, put that dratted mouse outside. If it's still there in the morning, then things are the same — no better, no worse. And if it runs free, it's going to die soon anyway, especially if the white cat finds it.'

'And there's no thimbles!' said Callum.

'Exactly. It'll be the end of it and of your troubles. That way it's nice and easy.'

'I'd prefer it.'

'Of course you've had your troubles. There could be an end to them soon. Things do change, you know. Look at me ... once there were children running round my feet. Their father's dead. We used to pull in on the verges by the roads. Had rain sting my face. We'd get moved along. Sold pegs by the dozen. Even made ointments from herbs, and I was known for it.'

'My mum does,' said Callum.

'Don't wish too hard for things to alter.... See what the morning brings. All things change soon enough, little brother, without you always wishing it.'

12

One after the other came sounds: first the sound of a woodpecker, then that of air rushing out of a pricked balloon, followed occasionally by a single note from a rusty tin whistle.

Gradually, as Callum awoke, he understood it was Mrs Delaney snoring. For a long time he lay there wondering at it and at how he had come to be there; thinking at one point, in a fever of disordered wakefulness, of Miss Probert smiling anxiously at him; of Maurice in a group of his friends, laughing, smelling of pencils, his fingernails full of dirt. Callum had never liked him.

Propping himself up, he looked out of the gypsy window. The ridge of the slope which sheltered them was crusted with moonlight. He was alert now, moving the curtains, each one no bigger than a handkerchief. Bravery was to be his only armour.

He wondered how Mrs Delaney's grandson managed with her snoring. Callum put the sound of it at the back of his mind.

He felt just as he had when returning the pig — except that his mission now was not to save the mouse, but to ensure its death. It did not bother him. He longed for the path to happiness.

∼

If he kept to the track for Barrow Farm, at least until daybreak, he would be all right. Mrs Delaney had left him in no doubt about the moor.

However long it took, he would find the white cat, and then he would come back and ask Mrs Delaney's forgiveness for the fright he would probably have caused her. He could not leave a message for her; he had no way of doing it. He even had difficulty in finding the cheese, let alone pencil and paper; but by moving slowly and feeling the shape of everything ahead of him, he was able to gather his clothes without sound and to move gradually to the door.

Once down the steps, he put his clothes on, but over his pyjamas, for it had grown cold. Soon, he felt the mouse move in his pocket. He had not doubted that it would be there; that it would be unharmed; that it would come to him.

∼

The track leading to Barrow Farm was quite distinct —
perhaps more so than it would have been during the
day — because of the shadows cast by the light of the
moon, and the winking stars.

The cat would, Callum felt sure, show up very well.
Looking to the left and to the right, he saw nothing; but
there was plenty of time. The hills billowed away into
the distance. It felt unreal — what he was doing — as if
he had stepped into a cupboard.

The dawn light started to thread into the eastern sky.
Ahead, the track appeared to fork. First one way, then
the other, seemed to disappear amongst rock and
heather in the uncertain light. Believing there to be
wheel-ruts in one track, Callum took that way.

Sometimes the mouse was in his pocket, at other
times ahead of him. Callum was aware of the passing
of time by watching the sky. Nothing, to the best of his
knowledge, had moved on the slopes.

The eastern sky reddened. The undersides of the
clouds on the horizon grew silver. Then the sun itself
rose as a great ball of fire. Already the hawks were in
the sky, and Callum could see for miles: the rough rock-
faces; the wild moor. No movement.

And there was no longer a track where he stood, nor
any sight of Barrow Farm.

~

Twice Callum thought he saw the white cat. Each time,
it turned out to be no more than the early sunlight
catching the quartz on outcrops of granite.

Marking the position of the biggest rock formation
he could see, he walked away from it as far as he dared

without losing sight of it; then he quarter-turned to the right and continued walking with great care, keeping the rock on his right and the same distance from himself, so that he was following a wide circle. This way, he thought, surely he would come across the track to Barrow Farm.

Then he saw other boulders, nearer ones, in the heather. The sun shone directly in his eyes. As hard as he tried, he kept losing sight of the boulder which was so vital to him, and focusing on another. He would sit down, shaking a little — it was noticeable when he stayed still — for much of his bravery had once more deserted him, as he tried to work out his position.

He felt better walking. He crossed a shallow stream of surface water. Although it only covered his feet, it was quite deep enough to stop the mouse. Callum walked on through it, with his heart thumping. But then, despairing, he had to stand still to allow the mouse — for his own comfort — to come out of his trouser leg, where it had just hidden.

~

Callum was certain enough that the dark line of hills on the skyline were those which sheltered Edgehill. Keeping these behind him — he had given up walking in a circle, and wished he had never started it — he searched among the low, clustered hills.

Many of them looked the same. He feared that some, indeed, were, and that he was merely walking over them again.

It was only when he clambered down, under the great blanket of cloud that covered Middlemoor, that he could see across the wild country which lay between him and home.

To start on such a journey would be madness. He could tell Victoria about this, and Maurice — about the fear of being in such a place; and about the urge to go on. His brain was beginning to work in a confused way. The endless walking and clambering, the shocks of feeling soft ground, the lack of food ... all this was affecting him. He longed for something warm. Tea, cocoa, then hot food: toad-in-the-hole, bacon, crackling.... Already Callum was making an endless list. Thinking of puddings.

Callum was not thinking properly. The weather had changed, as Mrs Delaney had said it would. More than anything else, it was the cold. Miss Probert, who often dealt with things outside the curriculum, had mentioned it. She had been talking about reasoning, thinking, the cognitive process — how dependent it was on outside circumstances. She had told them that cold slowed you down. That it could be quite peaceful, really, and so was doubly dangerous. She had also said that danger alerted you, quickened the thinking process. So being cold in a desperate situation was quite a struggle.

Callum found himself looking at rabbit tracks, passageways in the heather. A carcass of a rabbit that had been picked clean.

The moor across to Edgehill was impassable. The temperature had dropped. He was lost.

A voice in his head said: *There is no time for this!*

These were, he thought, his own inner words of warning.

The idea of survival quivered like a distant light. He said, 'It is not the mouse who is talking to me. I am my own master. I will get out of this!'

He was never sure if the mouse was with him. But he had only to stop, to wonder about it, and then he would feel it running about in his trouser leg. The longer he lay in the heather for rest, the more it would run on his leg. Sometimes when Callum wished for nothing more than to lie for a while, to be carried along in a great tide of sleep, the mouse ran about on his face and neck; once it whirled with great skill on the end of his nose.

Once more he was aware of a place in his imagination where he and the mouse could be. He fought against it, for he had no wish to mouse-talk, to reach an understanding with it. There could be no deals. No arrangements. Only death for it.

The moor would take care of it.

~

The sun had dipped behind the distant hills. The ridges blazed with silver. Once more Callum had struggled to his feet. Now and then he thought he might be walking in circles. He started trying to walk straight by walking towards the evening star — simply doing that, no matter where it took him. He did it for a short distance, then slumped behind a boulder.

He pulled out the cheese and unwrapped the plastic, slowly and with great difficulty. He had lost the sense of feeling in his hands. He could only just smell the cheese.

The memory of Miss Probert, and what she had said about people's olfactory senses, would not leave him. He thought, slowly, warmly, within himself, down long echoing corridors, of Miss Probert encouraging him ...

also of the hut and Phoebe smiling, and of the hams. Locked away, deep down in all this, was a voice which said, *'You've got to get out of this, Callum boy.'*

The mouse was on his hand. Callum ate as much cheese as he could. He had no hunger. He had forgotten all about food. He knew having the cheese would help.

He broke off small pieces of it and watched the mouse feed from his cupped hand.

Then, quite distinctly, due partly to his poor condition and partly to the relationship that he had always tried to deny, Callum heard this, in real mouse-talk:

'We need to get out of this, boy. Hereafter, in thankfulness to the Creator who guides us, I will never again wish for anything but ordinary cheddar cheese.'

There was a further communication from the mouse. It did not take the form of a message that was simply received and understood — something heard, then put aside. It stayed as a sound, something to which Callum struggled to turn. It was as if the mouse was speaking to him in his dreams. Then it would come again, very hard, as if pinching him: the words, *'Follow me!'*

~

The red sun raged in the western sky, and then the green and the violet turned to darkness. There was no moon, but gradually there appeared a covering of stars of such brightness and in such numbers as Callum had never seen before. For a strange, fearful moment, it made him wonder if he was still on the Earth.

Not for a moment, in all this, did Callum stop following the mouse. Its squeaks were at times almost continuous. The sound filled him, often breaking upon him like that of a bushful of sparrows rising in alarm.

Mrs Delaney; pig-stealing ... nothing mattered any more. It would be nice if he could buy a computer. But even that did not matter. There was peace here, the softness of a bird's nest.

Callum mouse-talked, *'I can hear your squeak as I have never heard it before. It entrances me.'*

And the mouse replied, *'I have lowered it from my usual squeak, which has a frequency of not much less than 23kHz, and which cats find so distasteful. I have done this for your convenience — so that you may hear it easily. I can do this because we are in a situation of extreme danger, and also due to my exceptional genes. Just follow me, boy.'*

Once or twice Callum's mind drifted. He imagined moor-people from long ago who had lived here — where, even then, no tree would grow — in settlements safe from the forests. Sometimes he thought there were rabbits conversing in the heather. Most of the time the squeaks prevented this nonsense. And all the way that Callum had come had been easy underfoot.

This was the journey's end. Ahead, in outline, were three huge slabs of stone, with another for a roof. Around them were three wild ponies of the moor.

Because snow had been forecast, a kindly farmer, who worried too much about most things, had left hay for the ponies. It was not common practice to do this, for they could have survived without it. Such conditions, for them, were not extreme.

Callum was in the hay, as deep as he could get. A pony had come back — all of them having, at first, turned away in fright. It was nuzzling Callum. He could smell its breath.

The mouse was at his side. Of this he was sure. He

was certain of little else. He could not think of anything in a focused way.

The sound of a helicopter, tracking over and over the moor, came into his consciousness and then out again, like an insect crossing a leaf. It had no meaning for him.

He was warm and safe and he could sleep. And this time the mouse did not prevent it.

13

The wind dropped. Clouds blanked out the stars. Snow fell.

It was as Mrs Delaney had said.

The day before, as soon as she had discovered that Callum was missing, she had done this:

She had struggled to the highest point overlooking the caravan, to get a good view of the moor, before searching towards Middlemoor. He was no older than her grandson. She felt a responsibility. Besides, in her moments of wakefulness in the night, she had wondered about the white cat. Should she have told him? Surely, after her warnings, he would not have been so foolish?

By putting her good leg forward and then pressing hard on her stick, she was able to climb quite rapidly. She had done it before.

She was about to turn when she saw him, a speck in the distance. She called, but it was no good. She could not follow. The pain was bad enough as it was.

Returning, she saw to the horse, giving it more hay.

She was so worried about the boy that she tried to think about something else.

For a year or two now, she had been unable to lift the shafts of her caravan. The horse was company, nothing more. They wouldn't be going anywhere. It was a reminder of what had been — that was all.

It was all over, the travelling life, she told herself. Things changed. Her son had done well, but he let her get on with it — the way she wanted to live. It was all dreams, now. But if only she had a mobile! The boy was in great danger.... It was her own fault. Her son had told her often enough.

She started on the track. She was anxious, walking much too quickly for her condition, driven by fear for the boy's safety.

By the time she was halfway to Middlemoor, she could neither move forward nor return. She was well wrapped up with shawls. She cried, but without too much fuss; not with self-pity, but as a refuge from the pain.

Late in the afternoon, the Calor-gas man came upon her.

Soon she was telling the police. They gave her tea. They were able to reach Aaron and Phoebe from the information Callum had given her. The helicopter was airborne by the time a taxi arrived to take her home.

That was yesterday.

~

Now the snow was falling, as Mrs Delaney had said it would. There was enough to whiten the moor. Nothing much else.

Callum was following the mouse again. There was the same spark of life, the same understanding between them, as there had been. Occasionally the mouse took refuge with him, where the snow had drifted. But if he changed the course, again the mouse would run ahead, where it was possible.

Over much of the ground, where the snow had first softened in the night, it had frozen crisp on the surface. This allowed the mouse to lead more easily. It found this wholly admirable.

Frequently the mouse asked Callum to have faith in his direction; or at least, Callum — in his state — imagined this to be so. He also believed — for he was nearly delirious and would have believed almost any-thing — that they would find safety and shelter once again. Of course, the thing was to find people. Anyone would do.

The snow had started again and was slanting into his face, and Callum, turning from it, saw Middlemoor bleak and huddled in the distance, its roofs whitened, the rest of it dark; for he had come right round the hills which previously had hidden it from view.

He should have turned back, of course. Several times he did so, only to find the way ahead suddenly becoming too dangerous without the mouse's company. Once he was sucked down in snow to his knees.

So he gave in again to the direction, to the *Follow me*. Again there was this feeling of lightness; of a light step. Of nothing happening outside. A feeling of under-standing how it was: how life was for the voles, and the rabbits and foxes on the moor, and all of them with room in their heads — Callum was thinking — for a little conversation.

He was well on the way to a bit of mouse-talking. He had also lost the feeling in his hands and much of his body.

The mouse said — and there was even a tone to it, for Callum believed it to be so — *'Because of my incredible genes, I have increased my homing capacity by another two miles. Ahead of us, four miles away, is our beloved Edgehill and our dear friends, the pigs. We will reach it by nightfall. I feel so much danger about me, it is vital I return to my box and the thimble without delay!'*

Callum tried to say clearly, *'Look! This would be the utmost foolishness. It is quicker to turn back.'* But he could feel the words drawn away into the wind.

Far away, a mere speck above the ground, beyond hearing, now and then vanishing from sight, a helicopter was flying low over the moor. It was too cold to think about it; to worry about anything at all.

Then, moving in the snow ahead of them — then still, and when it was still, almost unseen except for its eyes — was the white cat.

At first Callum did not believe it. He had waited so long.

Minute packed upon minute as if they were cards. He no longer tried to reason. He knew only that the quest was nearly ended. The delirium was lessened by the mouse running urgently up and down his leg. He could hardly feel it. But it helped.

The mouse had already taken up its position.

The squeaks were intense, directed with precision; many of them were beyond Callum's hearing, reaching a frequency of around 23kHz. They made no difference. Only when the mouse stared did the cat turn away.

The mouse ascended an outcrop of granite. Its great moment was near. Another burst of sound — perhaps it had not put enough effort into it; a stare, a harpoon that would tear its victim's brain! Then a leap into its fur!

The mouse whirred for a moment, more or less disappearing from sight, such was its speed. It was playing to the audience; to Callum. It was a failing it had, a problem with its personality.

Again it squeaked, expecting an easy victory. But this was not coming.

The boy was doing nothing to hinder the cat — nothing to frighten it away. And the mouse — although it had been disturbed by this, at first — began to take it as a compliment. The boy did not think interference necessary.

It was not that the mouse had serious doubts. It moved across the crisp surface of the snow, facing the cat squarely; and, sure enough, every time the mouse fixed its bright eyes — no bigger than grape seeds — the cat turned away.

A flurry of snow hid the mouse's eyes for a moment. So again it squeaked. So much effort was put into it that probably nothing like it had been heard by any cat before — that is, by any ordinary cat. It was a question of concentration. The mouse relished doing it.

It was a mistake. Just on the point of staring again, astounded by its own performance, the mouse received the first of the cruel whacks, which sent it crashing into a snow-laden clump of heather.

The mouse had been in a situation like this once before, in the boy's village. Being caught off guard. That, too, had been to do with the mouse's vanity. Then it had survived, as surely as it would now. Then, as now, the mouse had felt the flow of the Creator's love for living things ... and the boy's hands, as he had covered those wounds.

All of this was in a split second of awareness.

Also this: *The boy is still doing nothing.*

Another blow sent the mouse spinning up into the air. It felt as if an organ, its liver perhaps, was damaged beyond repair. It was overcome with shaking, hidden, for the moment, where it had fallen near the boy's feet.

The shivering stopped, as if its whole body had tightened. Stillness settled, holding it down like a claw. No wind sang in the heather. There was no herb on earth which could help with this. Still, the mouse would have liked the touch of the boy's hand.

Then the mouse called on the strength of its ancestors. It went haltingly to a stone. It was beginning to leave spots of blood in the snow.

On the stone, it stared at the cat once more. And once again, its natural enemy turned away.

The mouse needed to get the boy's attention. The boy was cold. It divided them. There had been no conversation between them since the cold had gone deep into the boy's body.

It was, however, the only chance.

Getting beyond the sensation of pain, it struggled to where Callum lay slumped, and whirred brokenly on the end of the boy's nose to get his attention. The mouse broke Callum's skin.

This failing, the mouse automatically dug deep into its store of knowledge.

It longed for home. Especially for the mouse-box. The delicious old dresses. The thimble! Yet what use would a thimble be here, without a mouse of its own kind to which it could be passed?

It was over.

The mouse toppled back into the snow. It laboured with the change from this life, being in a state of bodily chaos at its departure from it. It burrowed safely into dreams where cats would not harm it, nor the cold nights, nor the predators of the moor.

It was here, in these dreams where almost anything took shape as it wished, that it saw Callum again in the mind's eye, which meant that the boy was mouse-talking at last.

There seemed to be thimbles everywhere; but they were its fine drops of blood. The snow had turned to ermine.

The mouse had to get one message to the boy before there was an end to this nonsense — these imaginings. Ripping through its genetic structure was the desire for a truth. Not something the boy could not handle; not about creation and everything. It wasn't necessary.

It was about Change. It had hurt both of them.

For the mouse, it had been the end of the cheese made by the girl, the change to cheddar; but with it had come this bond of love between them. Had not the boy struggled with him across the moor towards home?

This is the shape of the truth which the mouse asked for, and which he was able to give to Callum: *The wind.... The wind over the moor, the wind blowing in the woods and in people's gardens amongst the wallflowers, and the wind at Finnegan's — all of it bringing Change, and carrying with it the seeds of new life and new beginnings.*

It was that. More or less.

Callum settled on the ground. He pushed the mouse with one hand towards the other. He was having a problem picking it up. The mouse was lying in the snow, sheltered by his two hands. Callum could not cry, for the cold had made this impossible.

The sound of rotor blades drummed down. The snow on the heather was beating away in a thousand crystals of light.

Out of the top of his head, he managed this: *'Forgive me, little mouse. Don't go, my dear friend!'*

He hardly felt the straps tightening on the stretcher. A voice through the brightness — there seemed to be a great deal of sunlight and snow — was saying, 'You're all right, sonny.'

And then a sleep.

14

Albert's send-off was a curious affair. Christ Church was full, as is so often the case at village funerals. Everyone there had known him — or, having sniffed the air, had been aware of him. This awareness had increased over the years with the installation of Number Two boiler, which, with its higher temperatures, had so often turned the most revolting carcasses safely into pigswill.

There had been times when it was feared that Albert might marry and produce a son and heir. But gradually it had become clear that he would remain a bachelor. So — as it was well known that his sister Lizzie could not stand the smell of pigs, let alone swill — this was seen as the end of an era.

Due to the ever-present smells, the villagers' olfactory

senses had been dulled, or rather focused on other, less frequent smells. It was, for instance, quite usual for them to be more or less unaware of the pigs, but able to recognise another smell — say, the smell of pancakes being fried, or of wallflowers. This kind of example had been used by Miss Probert to educate several generations of children, quite unnecessarily, on the olfactory sense.

But the swill-making always did hit them. Of late, the ostriches — mixed though they had been with yoghurt — had offended them. In vain they had hoped for an end to the ostriches. Were they whole ones? some had asked. If so, they reasoned, then surely the ostrich farmer would soon be going out of business? But it was far more likely, said those who feared the worst, that the never-ending supply of ostrich was from a highly successful farmer who was simply getting rid of unwanted bits and pieces, and that it would therefore go on for ever, or at least for as long as he farmed ostriches.

It was in an atmosphere of hopefulness — hope that here, at last, was an end to it — that the villagers had gathered for the funeral. Mr Parker of Parker & Parker, Solicitors, of Middlemoor, was also there. He had defended Albert against those people who, over the years, had gone to court to try and get judgements against the piggery for causing a nuisance. He was a thin man with a worried face and a rolled umbrella. He had grown fond of Albert. He would have gone to the service anyway, on account of this friendship.

Before it began, he had called to see Aaron.

'Everything is ready?' he had asked. 'It is a strange request, but there it is! Mr Finnegan had his little ways.'

It was a fine morning as the flower-decked cars

left the church. The undertaker, Maurice's father, was looking extra solemn. It was a splendid funeral. Lizzie — thinking that she was soon going to inherit — was not worried about the cost.

As instructed by Mr Parker — this being Albert's last wish — Aaron had lit Number Two boiler during the service. By the time it was over, and the mourners were gathering outside, the boiler was throwing out one of its richest smells for a long time. There was absolutely everything in it ... even pie-trimmings.

As luck would have it, a westerly wind blew. It was not too brisk, either. The smell filled the air in a nice, easy-going sort of way.

The pig-huts gleamed in the sun. There was a great sound of pigs, of snorting and squealing and wheezing. It was almost like an audience giving applause. High over the moor, a hawk lingered in a thermal. All was just as Albert would have wished.

There was no malice in this plan of his. It was his way of saying good-bye.

Later that day, Callum was discharged from hospital. So Phoebe, who had gone to collect him, had not been able to attend the funeral.

~

'You're welcome to stay on the farm until the will is read,' said Lizzie, afterwards. 'Then I can sell the pigs.... And of course you'll have to look after them in the meantime.'

'I'll do that,' said Aaron, 'but only out of respect for Albert.'

'But I want everything out of the cottage straight

away,' she said, a little sharply, 'including those hams. Then I'll lock it. And you can clean out those dreadful boilers, once and for all.'

'I dare say the sight of the hut doesn't bother you too much?' asked Aaron.

'You've got to live somewhere. Fancy the boy recovering in such a place!'

'When we leave here, it will be in a new caravan, I can tell you,' said Aaron.

'You did well out of Albert, then?' Lizzie said. 'And when you go, mind you don't leave a mess.'

'Is there anything else?' said Aaron, flushing with anger.

'Yes. Since you're still on wages, hose down those skips. I can't abide smells.'

~

That evening, as soon as Aaron had washed under the yard tap, he went to the hut.

'We'll soon be out of here, Callum boy,' he said.

'I'm all right,' said Callum listlessly.

'What we thought,' said Phoebe, 'was when you're up and about, we'd all go off and look at caravans. Now, how about that?'

'They've a wonderful range now,' Aaron said, 'better than when we bought the last one.'

'It was nice using Albert's electrics for a while,' she added.

The candlelight wavered. There were flowers under the Virgin. Aaron and Phoebe were sitting on the end of Callum's bed. Their faces looked fat with worry.

Phoebe burst out, 'Why did you do it? Why, Callum?'

She knew, of course. To get rid of the mouse — their way of life. And what was so hateful about it, for him, that he had risked his life to change it?

Then, without waiting for an answer, she said, 'You're going to have a scar on your nose, unless I'm much mistaken. How did it happen?'

All he said was, 'It must have got scratched.'

~

'We've always looked after him,' said Aaron one night, when Callum was asleep.

'And he's been sent to school, wherever we've been.'

'He's had too much schooling.'

'Don't start that again!'

But most of the time, while they waited for news of the pig sale, they were just glad that he was there with them. They still remembered the suspense when he had been lost. They had been so frightened, then, that they still had to tell themselves that now everything was all right. They often looked at him sleeping.

All that was wrong was the infection on the end of his nose. And the fact that they and Callum were talking very little to one another, when so much needed to be understood.

Phoebe had thrown out the mouse-cage, and, in doing so, had at last found her favourite tin thimble. And soon Callum was working amongst the pigs again. It was good for him, although he kept away from anything resembling a pig-thought.

He still found it difficult to talk about what it had been like on the moor; it meant thinking about the mouse. Perhaps he could tell his parents one day.

But he smiled when, out of the blue, Phoebe said, 'I'm proud of you, that you survived.'

There was a chance, then, to tell her. But he could not take it.

A moment later she added, 'It was the worst night of our lives.'

~

Victoria came to the piggery. 'I don't know what all the fuss is about,' she said, breathing hard through her nose. 'It's not bad.' Then: 'I read about you in the papers.'

'What papers?'

'The local one, of course. About you being rescued. Do you mean to say you didn't know you'd been in the news?'

'Mum may have said something. I didn't much care.'

'I'm sorry about Albert.'

'When do you start at Middlemoor Secondary?' asked Callum.

'Next week. What happened to your nose?'

Callum wanted to tell her, but was not certain if he was going to. This was for sure: he needed to speak to someone about the mouse — someone who would believe — without his heart breaking; someone who would not mind too much if it did.

15

The Ward family, including Katie, were seated in Mr Parker's office at Parker & Parker of Middlemoor.

'Miss Finnegan says she'll not set foot in the cottage,' said Mr Parker, 'although it is now hers, of course.'

'She would never have got used to the smell,' said Phoebe.

'It's not that, Mum,' said Callum. 'Although she would have noticed the smell less and less, the slightest whiff of pigs would have made her angry, because the olfactory lobe is part of the limbic —'

'Be quiet, Callum,' said Phoebe.

'It's what Miss Probert used to say.'

'I don't doubt it.'

'Albert knew she'd not consider it,' Aaron said, still looking flushed after hearing the will. 'He planned it so that there would still be a piggery after he'd gone. He always said she'd sell up if she had half a chance.'

'Well, I dare say he didn't want things to change — many of us don't; but I can assure you, Mr and Mrs Ward, that he also wanted to reward your loyalty in staying to look after him, when clearly the time had arrived — ahem — for you to leave.'

'I can't take it in — not yet, anyway,' said Phoebe. 'I'll have the electric, too.'

'You understand the farm and the cottage are hers?' Aaron nodded.

'You will pay a fair rent for the cottage — which I will agree with Miss Finnegan — and you will be able to stay there until such time as someone buys it. But,' said Mr Parker, 'you will show buyers over the cottage when it suits you, and only then. That is mentioned in the will. Mr Finnegan was most insistent that you should take the evening wind into account. I am to advise you, my dear sir, to show buyers around in the evening when it's been a warm day. The air tends to be — ahem! — *richer* then, as Callum already knows.'

'Do I?' Callum asked.

'The evening wind, boy! Mr Finnegan told you!'

'Oh, that. Yes, he did.'

'We'll still end up in a caravan if someone wants to buy it,' Aaron said.

'I'm afraid that is so,' said Mr Parker. 'But you'd keep it on the farm, no doubt?'

'Seeing that we'll be renting the land, yes,' said Aaron.

'And you can rent it for your lifetime, Mr Ward, or for as long as you want. You can put roots down, sir.'

'We owe it to Albert to stay,' said Phoebe.

'And, should the farm prosper, you would even

have the chance to buy it. It is all in here.' Mr Parker tapped the papers on his desk.

'Isn't she mad about it?' asked Callum.

'She's upset, yes,' smiled Mr Parker. 'But I have told her that a man in your position, Mr Ward, should get a mortgage.... It is the money she is interested in, not who owns it.'

~

Afterwards they lingered in Middlemoor.

'Are you coming home, Katie?' asked Callum.

'She's going to college, Callum, and she's doing all right where she is ... aren't you?' Phoebe said, looking at Kate.

'Yes, Mum,' said Kate quietly, pressing Callum's hand.

'Everything moves on, Callum boy,' said Aaron.

Kate said, 'There's nothing against visiting.'

Before returning to Edgehill, they took a taxi to Mrs Delaney's.

The wind was blowing in the heather. Callum kept his head down, not even seeing the horse. He looked up only at Mrs Delaney, into her eyes, when they had reached the caravan.

'So what's he left you, again?' the old lady asked.

'Not the cottage, not the farm — it's all to be rented. The farm for a lifetime, if we want it....' Aaron started to explain.

Callum said, 'Dad has got all the pigs.'

And Aaron added, 'Two hundred and fifteen sows, all saddlebacks, and just under half of 'em farrowed down, the rest dry; over three hundred piglets, and fifty gilts. And the boilers.'

'What are boilers good for?' asked Mrs Delaney.

'Remains,' Aaron said.

'Travelling's over, then?' she said.

∼

When the evening wind slid down the valley-sides, the smell, as usual, was at its strongest where the cottage stood.

If the weather was not right or the wind was coming off the moor, then buyers for the cottage were turned away.

One old gentleman said he did not mind the smell, so Aaron lit Number Two especially for him, and then he said he did.

But for most of the summer, the pig-smell rose high over the warm valley-sides. So Aaron would ask people to call back later, when it was a bit cooler. And then the soft breeze made the leaves flutter a little, bringing with it the gathered smells of the day.

The ostrich farmer seemed to be doing well. Sometimes there were more of the bits and pieces, sometimes fewer. There was rarely a boiling without them. The combination was terrific.

∼

For Callum, it was all changing.

At Middlemoor Secondary, Maurice had been picked on all term for being the son of an undertaker. This was after he had scorned Callum publicly because Number Two boiler had been lit after the service and his father had felt insulted.

And now Callum was telling the others to ease off — to give Maurice a break! Changes like this swept him along, leaving him on one island after another, so that sometimes he could scarcely recognise life as it had been.

Miss Probert, when they met once by accident, seemed older, thinner, than he had thought she was. They greeted each other politely.

At the new school, they'd heard he was a pig-talker.

Callum only shrugged.

'Your dad's a pig farmer?'

But to this, he nodded, smiling.

~

The villagers did not turn away any more. After a vigorous boiling from Number Two, they might look disgruntled. That was all.

Phoebe no longer walked to the Big Houses with her creaky willow basket.

The Wards' mousetraps were a thing of the past. The special genes had spread to neighbouring mice, but they were weakening all the time ... and perhaps there were fewer mice than there had been before.

And the light of pride was on the Ward family, and altered the look and touch of all things.

~

During that summer, Callum sometimes went into the empty hut. It smelled of resin where the pine-wood had heated up. It had started to rot in one or two places. If he shut his eyes he could just smell old mouse-smells, and so he thought, too — due to the process in the brain, which Callum understood — of his mother threading needles; of gathering kindling; taking that pig back.... How far away it all seemed!

He had told Victoria about the mouse. She, too, had changed. She had stood with him in the valley, and Finnegan's Wind had been blowing while he spoke.

Her face had changed in that one summer, or so it seemed. She had higher cheekbones than he had once thought, and her eyes had grown darker. Or was he just looking at her differently, from where they were now?

~

Once, in the woods, he was taken unawares, as if he was about to animal-talk with a mouse — to believe what came into his head. It had the same sleek kind of coat, and silvery eyes no bigger than grape seeds. But the moment passed.

Everything changed.

Except Finnegan's Wind. And that would blow for as long as there were pigs in the valley.

And should there be an end to the pigs, and to the boilers — although Callum could not foresee it — still it would be called Finnegan's Wind by those who remembered. Others would call it a wind from the west.

Also by John Wood

In a Secret Place

'Beguiling and magical'
The Irish Times

It was an adventure that coloured their lives —
that transformed the way they felt about one another and
about their families. And Alice, at least, was determined
to return to that secret place, to experience again
the feeling of magic and half-dream.
But how to find the right path back?

Together, Alice, Yanina, Paul and Benjamin went on an
expedition to the woods. They didn't have much
in common, but they had this, at least:
none of them got on with their parents....

And then, quite suddenly, the special path
led them to the secret place.

'[Readers] will be held by the book's narrative power —
and the warmth and generosity of its heroine.'
The Times Educational Supplement

'Sensitive ... imaginative ... highly recommended.'
Consumer Choice

ISBN 0-86327-399-8

New from Wolfhound Press

The Alphabet Network

by Jeanette Bresnihan

It's the middle of the twenty-first century,
and Europe has become a wasteland —
there are no plants or flowers, no children are being born.
Only Ireland is still safe, fertile and beautiful.

Somewhere in the West of Ireland lives Katie's grandfather.
She and her little brother Tom have to find him,
to give him the mysterious box their father entrusted to
them before he died. They have help from the secret
Alphabet Network, Patch the handsome farm-boy,
Madame Bonbon the circus fortune-teller,
and many others. But the terrifying man in white
and the beautiful, sinister Miss Craven are desperate
to get their hands on the box — at any cost.

And Katie and Tom don't realise
quite how much depends on their journey....

A gripping, atmospheric book,
with a colourful cast of characters and a powerful message.

ISBN 0-86327-833-7